Zombies!

The zombie moves with cautious ease, using the greater reach of its spear to full advantage. Alynn realizes he would have stood no chance against the skilled warrior whose shadow now serves the Darklord. He tries to take advantage of the creature's slower reflexes and decaying strength to dart in and strike a disabling blow, but the spearpoint always seems to block his way. Slowly, the living man is forced back. Finally he finds his calves pressed against the low wall of the well.

Another lunge of the spear and the point tangles in the cleric's robe, nearly pushing him into the open well. A wild swing of his mace forces the zombie back. Alynn swings again, aiming to smash a hand, only to discover the hand gone and the spear once again driving toward his ribs. His loose cassock again tangles the spearpoint...

Ace Fantasy Books by Bill Fawcett

The SwordQuest™ Series
QUEST FOR THE UNICORN'S HORN
QUEST FOR THE DRAGON'S EYE
QUEST FOR THE DEMON GATE

QUEST FOR THE ELF KING
(Coming in January 1987)

SWORDQUEST

Quest for the DEMON GATE

BILL FAWCETT

ACE FANTASY BOOKS
NEW YORK

This book is an Ace Fantasy
original edition, and has never
been previously published.

QUEST FOR THE DEMON GATE

An Ace Fantasy Book/published by arrangement with
the author

PRINTING HISTORY
Ace Fantasy edition/September 1986

All rights reserved.
Copyright © 1986 by Bill Fawcett.
Cover art by Neal McPheeters.
Maps by Jerry O'Malley.
Illustrations by Todd Hamilton.
This book may not be reproduced in whole or in part,
by mimeograph or any other means, without permission.
For information address: The Berkley Publishing Group,
200 Madison Avenue, New York, New York 10016.

ISBN: 0-441-13807-1

"SwordQuest" and the stylized SwordQuest logo are
trademarks belonging to The Berkley Publishing Group.

Ace Fantasy Books are published by The Berkley Publishing Group,
200 Madison Avenue, New York, New York 10016.
PRINTED IN THE UNITED STATES OF AMERICA

*Humbly dedicated to Beth,
for all her patience.*

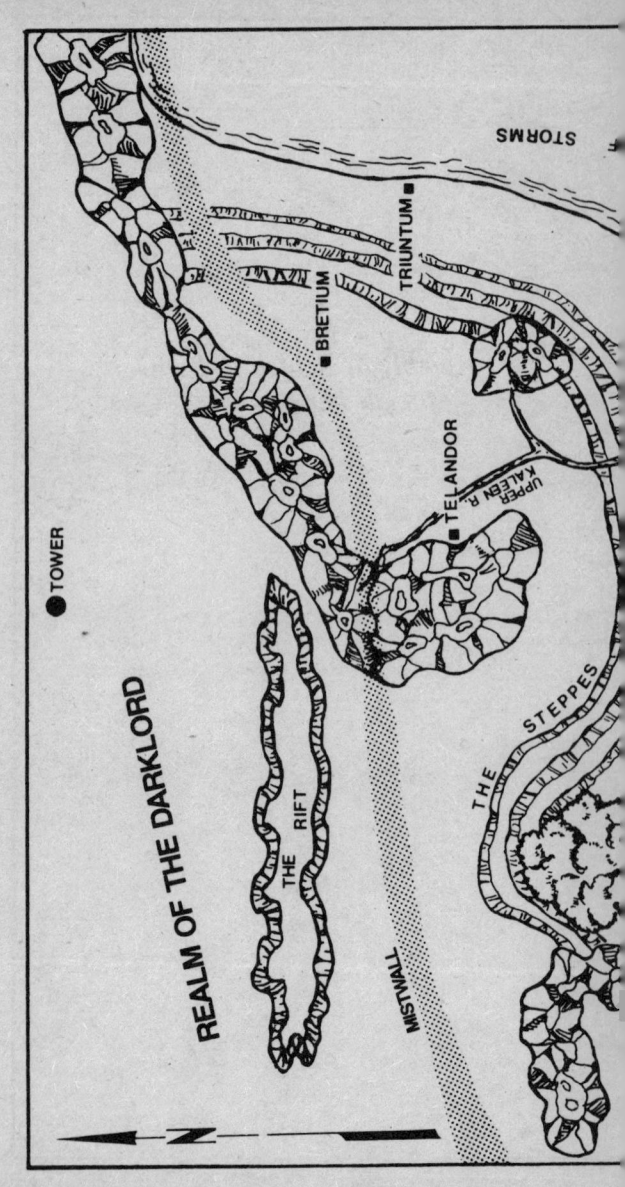

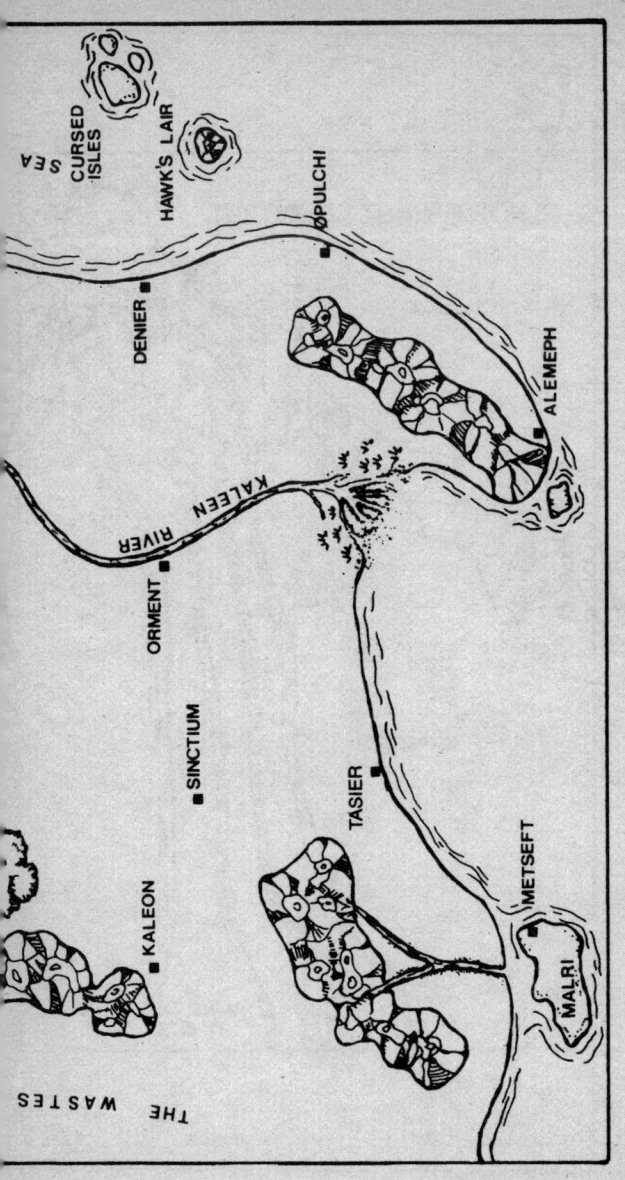

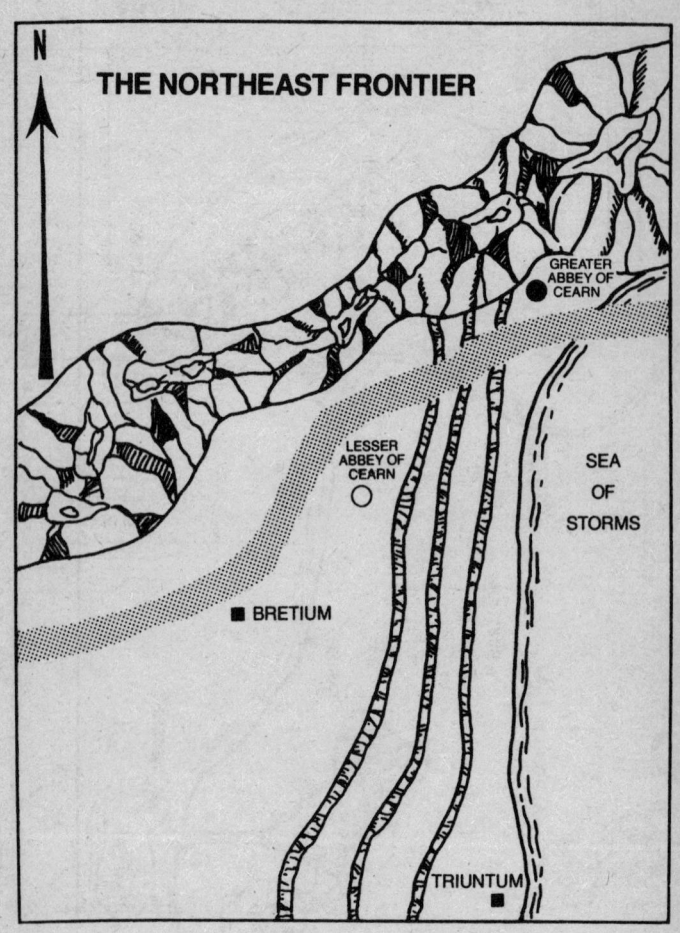

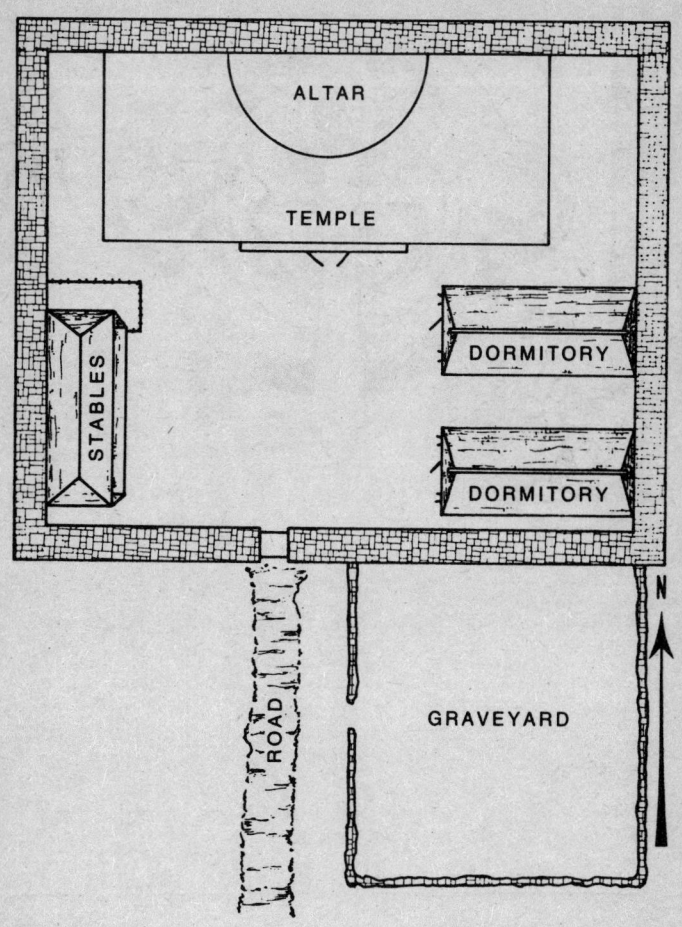

What Is a Role-Playing Novel?

A novel tells a story, hopefully in such a way as to entertain the reader. In a role-playing game the story is created by the actions of the player's characters. SwordQuest role-playing novels are adventures wherein you, the reader, help to create the story. As the reader you will make decisions and, by means of simple rules included in this book, see how the results of your decisions affect the Hero.

Unlike most "choose your path" adventures, SwordQuest novels strive to present more than just a random description of hazards. Your choices will be more successful if you keep your quest in mind. You will always be given at least a hint of the best action to take when faced with any decision. SwordQuest novels are also intended to be what, in another time, would have been described as "a rousing good tale of adventure"—at least as much fun to read as to play.

A SwordQuest novel is divided into sections rather than chapters. A section may be only a few sentences long, or it may continue for several pages. The section number, rather than a page number, is shown at the top of each page. This will help you to find the next section more easily. A section will contain the events that stem from a particular decision or result of a combat. You will be directed to the correct section whenever one of these situations occurs.

Quest for the Demon Gate tells the tale of Alynn, a devout cleric thrust into an adventure filled with undead and enchanted monsters. You will make decisions about what Alynn should do, and you will fight his battles for him. Whether you win or lose will affect the outcome of the story. A Hero who is a prisoner or dead is no longer in a position to complete his quest.

This book begins with an easy-to-use role-playing system. Here you will be concerned with how strong or how big your enemy is, the use of magical items, and even the Hero's Dexterity and Intelligence. There is also a simple method for creating your own Hero to adventure in place of Alynn. At least one six-sided dice and a pencil are needed. (The words "six-sided dice" are abbreviated as "D6." The number ahead of the "D6" tells you how many six-sided dice to use. "3 D6" means you will roll three six-sided dice and add the total. Three six-sided dice are often used in these rules, and it will save you time if you roll three at once.)

Finally, this role-playing novel is written so it can be easily played with the more complicated fantasy role-playing games. These include TSR, Inc.'s popular DUNGEONS & DRAGONS® role-playing game.

THE HERO

Only the bravest and most talented survive as Heroes or Wizards in the SwordQuest role-playing novels. These are the characters who brave dank dungeons and battle fearsome beasts. While each book is written about a different Hero, you can use a favorite Hero from another book in place of the one presented. All you need to do is read to yourself the name of your Hero where "Alynn" appears. This can be a character from your current fantasy role-playing campaign or one you create just to use with the SwordQuest novels. If you have a D&D character, you will find most of the numbers transfer directly. By successfully completing the adventures in different SwordQuest books, it is even possible to have your Hero grow more skillful.

Every Hero has six values which describe what the Hero is like. These values show the Hero's STRENGTH, INTELLIGENCE, WISDOM, CONSTITUTION, DEXTERITY, and CHARISMA. An additional value, the HIT POINTS of the Hero, shows how much damage the Hero can take and continue adventuring.

The beginning of each SwordQuest adventure includes the RECORD SHEET for the Hero who appears in the novel. The record sheet for Alynn, the Hero of *Quest for the Demon Gate*, appears on page 10. On this record sheet you will record all of the Hero's values, any magical items he or she starts adventuring with, and a description of anything unusual about the character. It may be important if your Hero is afraid of heights or hates lizards.

WHAT THE NUMBERS REPRESENT

STRENGTH. This value measures how strong the Hero is and, if high enough, can give the Hero extra hit points. Being very strong means you can do more damage when you hit. This is called a Strength bonus. These bonuses are:

Strength of 16	1 extra hit point of damage
Strength of 17	2 extra hit points of damage
Strength of 18	3 extra hit points of damage
Strength of 19	4 extra hit points of damage
Strength of 20	5 extra hit points of damage

It is possible to have a Strength value over 18 only by the use of magical items.

Let's take a look at a SwordQuest character named Yeng the Barbarian. He is a Hero with a Strength of 16 trying to hit a Dragon with his sword. Normally a sword would cause damage equal to the number rolled on one six-sided dice. In this case a 4 is rolled. Because Yeng is so strong, 1 more point is added to the number rolled (4 + 1 bonus = 5) for a total of 5 hit points of damage. Five points are subtracted from the original 20 hit points the Dragon started with, which means the Dragon has 15 hit points left.

INTELLIGENCE. This value shows how good the Hero is at figuring out puzzles and also how tough the Hero's mind is when attacked by ESP, illusions, or hypnosis.

WISDOM. Sometimes fate or the god—or whatever intervenes in the fantasy universe the Hero is adventuring in—likes the Hero. This may be because the Hero is a faithful follower of the god or simply for no good reason at all. The value for Wisdom is a measurement of the closeness of the Hero to those powers that rule his universe. A high value, over 16, means the Hero may be able to call for miracles and actually get them. A low value, under 6, means he is really on his own.

CONSTITUTION. This shows how well the Hero can endure under stress. A Hero with a high Constitution value can swim farther or run longer distances than one with a low value.

DEXTERITY. Having a high value for Dexterity is important. This value measures how fast and also how coordinated the Hero is. A successful acrobat or magician will have a high Dexterity. A Hero with a very low Dexterity is commonly referred to as a "klutz."

CHARISMA. It is helpful for the Hero to be able to get people or even monsters to do what he wants. This may be to sell him a horse or simply to convince the Dragon not to eat him. The higher the Hero's Charisma, the better the Hero is at getting information or convincing men to follow him into battle. Julius Caesar had a high Charisma. A very good-looking person will also have a high Charisma value. Robert Redford and Miss America have really high values for their Charisma, probably 18s.

HIT POINTS. The value you roll for hit points shows how tough the Hero is. A Hero with only 10 hit points is fairly easy to kill. A Hero with 24 can survive a bite from a Dragon and keep on fighting. When a monster succeeds in "hitting" a Hero, the damage is subtracted from the number of hit points the Hero has left. When all of a Hero's hit points have been lost, the Hero is probably dead or at least unable to continue the adventure. Heroes with a high skill level will have more hit points.

If your Hero dies, just roll up a new Hero and try again. Even the most powerful Hero can be killed by rolling too many high dice for the monsters or making a few wrong decisions. You should learn a lot from each Hero, even if he or she dies before completing the adventure, enabling your next Hero to do much better.

SKILL LEVEL

The more you do something, the better you get at it. This is true for playing chess, sports, or even adventuring. In your first SwordQuest book you should start the Heroes you create with a skill level of zero. They are basically inexperienced at adventuring but have been trained in the use of arms and tactics. Alynn, the Hero given in *Quest for the Demon Gate,* is such a Hero. He is a simple cleric who suddenly finds himself thrown into conflict with the powerful forces of the evil Darklord.

As your Hero completes the adventures in each SwordQuest novel, he gains one more level of skill. This reflects his greater ability as a seasoned warrior and the benefits he acquires by having faced such fearsome foes before in combat (ho-hum, another Dragon?). In game terms the skill level a Hero has is added as a bonus on every combat dice roll. The higher the skill level of the warrior, the more likely he is to hit an opponent. A Hero who has completed two SwordQuest adventures will be a skill level two warrior. A Hero who has completed three role-playing novels will be at skill level three. For instance, suppose the Hero can hit a skeleton with a total of 12 or better on three six-sided dice. Attacking first, he only rolls a total of 10. As he is just a skill level zero warrior, this would miss. Given a lot of luck, the Hero will complete a few quests. He will then be a skill level two warrior. As a skill level two warrior, a +2 is added to his roll, giving him the total of 12 needed to hit the skeleton. You would then roll normally to determine the damage he did. No extra hit points of damage are gained just because the Hero has a higher skill level.

MAGICAL ITEMS

Many different magical items are found in the pages of the SwordQuest novels. In most cases these can be taken by the Hero to use later in the adventure. These magical items range from extra-sharp swords and potions with amazing powers to wands that shoot fireballs. A few are even cursed and will have strange and terrible effects on anyone using them.

Most magical items are simply improvements on everyday weapons or armor. These may have been enchanted by a Wizard or forged by demons. The extra power of these magical items is given in a value such as "+2." This is the bonus you add to the three dice you roll to see if a hit was made. The bonus is added to the roll if the item is a weapon or subtracted from the "to hit" roll if the magical item is a suit of armor or a shield.

Magical weapons also do extra damage. A magical weapon does 1 extra hit point of damage for every point it is enchanted. A +2 sword will add 2 to the "to hit" total—and will do 2 extra points of damage if a hit is rolled.

Other magical items will enable your Hero to fly, jump over tall buildings, or do just about anything. What the magical item does will be described in the adventure. You can never use a magical item, except for weapons, healing potions, or armor, unless using it is one of the options at the end of the section. Weapons and armor may be used in all combat situations. Most magical items can be used many times, but a few can be used only a limited number of times. When you are using an item that has limited uses, you will be told to keep track of how many times you use it on the record sheet.

Magic is very powerful. Too much magic in one area cancels out the abilities of all the magical items. Because of this a Hero or Wizard is limited in the number of magical items he can carry. Every character in a SwordQuest adventure may have only five magical items. If a sixth item is found, you have to decide on the item that will no longer be carried. This item is lost from play. Do this by simply erasing the item off the record sheet.

Once a magical item has been thrown away, it is lost forever. You cannot go back and pick it up later. All magical potions can be used only once. Using a potion is the same as throwing it away, and it should be erased from your record sheet. Whenever you use a potion, follow the instructions in the section you are reading. Except for the healing potions, which may be used whenever you feel it necessary (but only one time per potion), you can't use a potion unless the option is given to your Hero at the end of the section. If the option is given, but you have already used the potion, you cannot choose that option.

ARMOR

The best of armor, whether a shiny suit of plate or a bulletproof vest, is uncomfortable. Yet hundreds of thousands of soldiers throughout history have worn it. Having on a nice thick chain-mail coat or carrying a shield will make it harder for an opponent to successfully hit the Hero. The type and amount of armor a Hero is wearing will be listed on the record sheet. In most cases a Hero should wear at least chain mail, and he may carry a shield.

If the Hero loses the shield he is carrying, +1 should be added to every "to hit" roll by whatever attacks him. If the Hero is not wearing his chain-mail armor, +3 should be added to the roll for all his opponents "to hit" him. This will reflect how much easier it is to harm an unarmored man. If both are lost, a total of +4 should be added.

A Hero could start the novel wearing a piece of magical armor, or he could find one during his travels. The value of the magical armor is shown by how much more difficult it becomes for the Hero to be hit. This has the same effect as subtracting the armor's bonus from the "to hit" total of the attacker.

A +1 shield makes it 1 point harder for the monster to hit whoever is using it. If an Orc could hit Yeng on a total of 10 before, the same Orc would need a total of 11 if the Barbarian was carrying the +1 shield.

Only one magical shield and magical suit of armor can be used at a time. Each individual piece of this armor counts as a magical item. If the Hero finds a second magical suit or shield, you will have to decide which one he is going to wear. Extra suits can be carried in the Hero's pack, but there's no bonus given for having them if the Hero is attacked.

CREATING A HERO

To create your own Hero, make a copy of the blank record sheet provided. Permission is given for you to photocopy this page only. You then need to complete the following steps:

1. Roll three six-sided dice (or one six-sided dice three times and add the result) to get a value for each of the six qualities that describe the Hero. For example, if you roll a 4, 5, and 6 for a total of 15, the value of the Strength of your new Hero will be 15. Record these on the record sheet on page 10 or on a separate sheet. An average roll is between 9 and 12.

2. Roll 4 D6 (four six-sided dice) to determine the number of hit points your Hero will begin with. Record this also on the record sheet.

3. All new Heroes begin with a skill level of zero. Put a "0" on the record sheet for the new Hero's skill level. In some SwordQuest adventures the Hero supplied will be an experienced warrior and so begin at a higher level. This will reflect the Hero's greater abilities and enable him to survive in combat with more deadly opponents.

4. If the new Hero is given any magical items, these should be listed now. The Hero presented in a SwordQuest novel will normally have a few enchanted items which will aid him in his efforts. Others will become available as loot or gifts from other characters in the novel. The blank area on the record sheet allows

you to keep track of such items as food or gold when they are important for playing the adventure in the novel. If such items are given to the Hero described in the SwordQuest adventure, you will need to give them to the characters you roll up as well.

THE RECORD SHEET

Hero _____

Strength _____   Hit Points _____

Intelligence _____ Magical Items _____

Wisdom _____   1. _____

Constitution _____ 2. _____

Dexterity _____   3. _____

Charisma _____   4. _____

Skill Level _____   5. _____

Other items carried:

_____

_____

_____

_____

_____

_____

_____

_____

_____

COMBAT

Many times in a SwordQuest role-playing adventure novel the Hero will have to battle terrible monsters or humans. To determine who wins a combat, follow these rules:

Unless otherwise stated, the Hero always gets to act first. This may be to take a swing at the monster, use a magical spell, or even run away.

For every opponent four values are given.

The first is the total that has to be rolled on 3 D6 to hit the Hero.

The second is the total the Hero, using a nonmagical weapon, needs to hit the monster.

The third is the number of hit points the monster begins the battle with. When the Hero has reduced this number to 0, the monster is dead and the Hero has won.

The fourth is the amount of damage the monster does to the Hero every time it hits him.

You can run away only when that option is offered at the end of the section. In many cases this will mean the opponent will get at least one attack on the Hero's unprotected back. There is also the chance you will not be able to escape from the faster monsters.

COMBAT SEQUENCE

The steps you follow in a combat are:

1. First you roll 3 D6 and add the total to see if the Hero is able to hit the monster with his weapon. You then add to this total any bonus if the Hero is using a magical weapon and subtract the value of any magical armor the opponent may be wearing. If your final total is the same as or larger than the "needed to be hit" value for the monster, the Hero has "hit."

If the Hero hits the monster, you then determine how many hit points of damage he did. Roll the number of dice listed for the weapon the Hero is using and add to it any bonus the Hero might have because he is very strong or is using a magical weapon. These hit points are subtracted immediately from the monster's total as listed in the section. If the result is a value of 0 or less, the monster has been slain.

2. If the Hero fails to slay the monster on the first swing, the monster has a chance to fight back. Again you roll 3 D6, but this time for the monster's attack. You then must subtract from this total any magical bonus for enchanted armor the Hero is wearing. If the resulting total is the same as or larger than the value given for "to hit the Hero," the monster has successfully caused damage.

To determine the damage done to the Hero, roll whatever dice are listed as "Damage." The total rolled for damage is then subtracted from the total number of hit points currently listed for the Hero on the record sheet. If the Hero's hit points reach 0, he is dead. If the Hero has any hit points left, he may continue with the battle or with the adventure.

3. One attack by both the Hero and his opponent is called a "round" of combat. Each round would take about six seconds in real life. If both the Hero and any of the monsters he is fighting are still alive, another round of combat is fought. Combat always lasts until either the Hero is killed, the monster is killed, or someone runs away. Unless healed magically, your Hero cannot regain the hit points lost in a battle. Ten small wounds can kill a Hero as surely as one massive attack.

There will be times when the Hero is facing more than one opponent. How to handle this will be given in the section where it occurs.

Once the combat is over, turn to the section listed for the result and continue the adventure.

The Sequence of Combat:
    First Round
1. Hero attacks, runs, talks, and so forth
2. Monsters attack
    Second Round
3. Hero attacks
4. Monsters attack

Third and Other Rounds
Continuing, Hero then Monster, until resolved.

SPECIAL ACTIONS

There will be times in a SwordQuest role-playing adventure novel when you will have the choice of making your Hero attempt a difficult feat. This may be to climb a slippery wall, sneak quietly past a guard, or even hold his breath for a very long time. The values you rolled for your Hero (or those given on the record sheet) are used to determine if the Hero succeeds. You will be told in the section which characteristic to use. If the attempt requires persuasion, Charisma is used. If the situation calls for acrobatics, Dexterity is used. If you are hoping for a miracle to save your Hero, Wisdom is the key value.

Whenever such an attempt is made, you will be told to roll 3 D6 and compare the total to one of the values. If the number you roll is the same as or less than the value on the record sheet, the Hero succeeds. If the total of the three dice is greater than the value given, the Hero fails and must suffer the consequences.

YENG THE BARBARIAN

To give an example of "rolling up" and playing a new Hero let's use Yeng. He is the sixth son of a chief and on his own for the first time. You also decide Yeng is young, six feet tall, and swarthy. He has black hair, which is always curling up over the edges of his helmet, and wears the emblem of a coiled snake. These are just "background" and will not affect play. Rolling 3 D6 for each of Yeng's values, we get the following results, which are noted on the record sheet:

Strength—Here you roll well, two 5s and a 6 for a total of 16. Yeng is not only very strong, but he is strong enough to do an extra hit of damage every time he hits a monster.

Intelligence—An average roll here. Yeng ends up with an Intelligence value of 11. While not a genius, Yeng is bright enough to be a good warrior.

Wisdom—You don't roll as well here. With a Wisdom value of only 6, Yeng is not likely to be very good at miracles. Nearly every time he tries to invoke his favorite deity, he forgets half the words.

Constitution—The three dice roll for the values 6, 6, and 5, making Yeng a very sturdy warrior. With a total value of 17, he never seems to get sick and has a cast-iron stomach. With his tough constitution Yeng is probably able to fight longer, drink more, and swim farther than anyone he knows.

Dexterity—Rolling a 3, 2, and 4 gives Yeng a total of 9. This means his Dexterity is below average. He can handle a sword without hurting himself and can dodge most blows but should probably not try juggling sharp objects.

Charisma—Really bad luck here. Your three dice rolls of 2, 1, and 3 add up to 6, way below average. Yeng may find he looks like the type merchants feel they have to cheat, and he will need quite a reputation before men will follow him into battle. Having a Charisma value of 6 may also mean Yeng is simply ugly or has some other particular flaw—perhaps a squeaky voice or a scar across half his face. (This could be why he wears a beard.)

Hit Points—You roll four dice here for the values 2, 4, 4, and 6: a respectable total of 16. Nothing is likely to kill Yeng with just one blow. He can take considerable damage and keep on fighting.

Skill Level—In this example, Yeng is just starting off as a Hero. He has a skill level of zero, which means his "to hit" bonus for experience is 0. This is the same as no bonus.

INTRODUCTION

Once you have "rolled up" your Hero, the next step is for you to assign him any magical items, weapons, or special objects. Yeng starts with nothing but a potion for running faster and a magical goblet that prevents drunkenness. Note these on his record sheet and he is ready to begin the adventure.

Yeng normally wears his chain mail and carries the biggest shield he can find. Quaffing his fourth Celtic whiskey, he decides the chain mail is too bulky to wear while serenading his current infatuation, the Duke's daughter (probably an unfortunate choice, as part of Yeng's low Charisma value is due to his tendency to sing off key). On the way to the Duke's castle Yeng is confronted by a Troll. Normally a Troll needs a 12 to hit Yeng when he is wearing his chain mail and carrying his shield. Since Yeng left his chain mail at home, he now has only his shield. This means the Troll receives a bonus of +3, so only needs to roll a total of 9 on 3 D6 to hit him. Yeng is in trouble.

Somehow our Hero survives his encounter with the Troll. (He did have a potion for fast running.) Yeng returns home and finds he inherits a +1 longsword from his father. Later, rushing to the sounds of a fair maiden in distress, our intrepid Barbarian rounds the corner and is faced with an Orc. Pulling out the enchanted sword, Yeng lets loose with a battle cry and tries to hit the Orc. Normally Yeng needs a roll with a total of 11 to successfully do damage to an Orc. The total of the three dice you rolled for Yeng is a 10. Because Yeng is using the magical sword, you add 1 to the 10 and Yeng has an 11 for his final "to hit" total. Rolling a second time for damage, you roll a 5 on one six-sided dice. The Orc began with only 3 hit points, so this is enough to kill it. Yeng slices into the Orc with a mighty blow. The battle is over.

If the Orc had been wearing magical +1 armor and Yeng had been carrying a normal sword, you would have had to subtract 1 from the original dice throw of 10, leaving a total of 9. Yeng would have missed. Actually the sword might have hit the shield or armor, but not hard enough to hurt the Orc.

Yeng hit the Orc with his +1 longsword. Normally the number rolled on 1 D6 would be how many hit points of damage Yeng does to the hapless Orc. A 4 is rolled. Because Yeng was using his +1 longsword, 1 extra hit point of damage is added. This means a total of 5 hit points is subtracted from the Orc's current total. If Yeng had been using a +2 magical sword, the bonus would have been 2 and the final total 4 + 2, or 6.

Having saved the maiden, Yeng is given a treasure map by her grateful father. Considering Yeng's obvious greed, the father asks to hold his magic sword until the map is returned. Having a below-average value for Intelligence, the Barbarian agrees. His low Charisma value makes it likely her father gave Yeng the map to get him out of town.

Following the map, Yeng the Barbarian enters a cave, which is about twenty feet deep and ten feet high. On the far wall there is a door that his treasure map says opens to a room containing a bag of gold. Guarding the door is another Orc with a sword. Being both brave and more than a bit greedy, Yeng draws a nonmagical sword and attacks.

THE ORC

To Hit the Hero: 13   To Be Hit: 11   Hit Points: 4
Damage with Sword: 1 D6

Yeng attacks first. To see if he hits the Orc, you roll 3 D6 for the values 2, 3, and 4—a total of 9. Even with Yeng's strength bonus of +1, the final total of 10 is not high enough to hit. Yeng swings and the Orc ducks under the whistling blade.

Now it is the Orc's chance to swing back. You roll three dice for the Orc's attack and they are 3, 5, and 6—a total of 14, which is enough to hit Yeng. As the damage the Orc does is listed as "1 D6," you must roll one six-sided dice and subtract the number rolled from Yeng's original 16 hit points. You roll a 2, so you cross out the 16 hit points Yeng had on the record sheet and replace it with the 14 hit points the Hero has left.

This is the end of the first round of combat. Looking at the options you can have Yeng either stay and fight, or flee. You decide Yeng needs the money and stays in the battle.

To begin the next round you roll three dice for Yeng's second attack. This time Yeng must be mad, for you roll 6, 6, and 5 for a total of 17. This is far more than the 11 Yeng needs to hit the Orc, even without the Hero's strength bonus. You then roll the damage listed for an ordinary sword, which is 1 D6. This roll is a 3. To this you add the 1 hit point of extra damage Yeng does because he is so strong. This gives a total of 4 hit points you now subtract from the Orc's total. Since the Orc only had 4 hit points to start with, the result is 0. With no hit points left, the Orc is slain by Yeng and the battle is over.

Yeng has fought his way past the Orc guard and opens the door to the treasure. Stepping through the door, the Barbarian is nearly cut in half by a giant blade swinging like a pendulum across the center of the room. He can see the bag of gold resting on a table on the other side of the pendulum.

You are given the choice at the end of the section to either give up on the gold and continue on Yeng's journey, or try to get past the blade and grab the gold. You decide to take the option listed for dodging past the pendulum. In the section you turn to, it says you must roll a total lower than Yeng's Dexterity value for him to safely dash past the blade. Yeng has a Dexterity of 9, which isn't very high, but you roll lucky. The dice total only 8, so Yeng successfully slips past the swinging blade.

Turning to the section listed for successfully dodging the blade, you read Yeng has gained 100 gold pieces. You also discover there is only one way in or out of the room. Yeng will have to dodge past the blade once more to get back out with his loot. Adding the 100 gold pieces to the record sheet, you prepare to roll once more against Yeng's Dexterity value.

WEAPONS CHART

Weapon	Damage	Limitations
Arrow	1 D6	
Battle Axe	1 D6	
Club (large)	1 D6	
Dagger	1 D6 − 1	
Dart	1 D6 − 2	
Flail	1 D6 + 1	
Halberd	1 D6 + 2	use on foot only
Hammer	1 D6	
Lance	2 D6	use from horseback
Mace	1 D6	
Pike	1 D6 + 1	use on foot only
Spear	1 D6	
Staff	1 D6	use on foot only
Sword, long	1 D6	
Sword, short	1 D6 − 1	
Sword, two-handed	1 D6 + 1	use on foot only
Trident	1 D6	

A value of plus or minus after the damage is added or subtracted from the number rolled. If the damage resulting is 0 or less, no hit points are lost.

CLERICAL MAGIC

A cleric is the active representative of any deity or spiritual power in the fantasy world. He is granted by his deity the ability to use spells. The deity can be beneficent or evil. It can be a minor godling or even a powerful demon. The lesser gods, perhaps having nothing more important to do, are often active in the affairs of men. A cleric can be a shaman in a mud hut or the high priest of a marble temple.

Skill levels for clerics are handled in the same manner as those for fighters. In *Quest for the Demon Gate,* Alynn is a cleric who follows Cearn, a minor deity concerned with refuge during times of peril. This being a period of relative peace, Cearn is worshiped mostly by those who choose to enter his Sanctuaries. A Sanctuary of Cearn protects a man from all powers outside it, even the power of the King. To gain this complete protection the individual must forsake all earthly wealth and pledge to devote his life to the service of Cearn. Temporary shelter and food are freely given to anyone who enters a Sanctuary, but he must leave by the next sunrise.

Clerics, as men of the spirit, are limited in battle effectiveness because they must not shed blood. They cannot fight monsters very effectively because they are not well trained in combat. Clerics are also limited in the weapons they may use. Any weapon with a sharp edge or point is forbidden, including swords, halberds, and arrows.

One of the greatest advantages gained by clerics is the use of "miracles," or clerical spells. The higher the level of the cleric, the greater number and more powerful the miracles he has available. You should remember, though, that the availability of the spell does not guarantee a cleric will be able to use it effectively. A dice roll is required each time you attempt to use a spell.

The cleric's ability to use these spells is measured by his Wisdom value. The higher the Wisdom the more likely the cleric is to be successful with the spell you choose to use. To use a clerical spell you first choose a spell from those listed at the end of the section. Not all spells will be listed each time. You then roll 3 D6 (three six-sided dice) and add the total rolled. If this value is the same as or lower than the cleric's Wisdom value, the spell was successful. If the total rolled is greater, the spell fails, having a negative or no effect. Any spell can be attempted only once. Even if unsuccessful, the spell is lost for the rest of the adventure. You can take the same spell more than one time. For example, Alynn could choose to take three Spirit Hammer spells. Each one could be attempted once.

For example, Artus Castle is a cleric being chased by a skeleton. He turns and tries to cast a Turn Undead spell on it. Artus has a Wisdom value of 13 and rolls a total of 10 on 3 D6 (three six-sided dice). The spell is successful, and the skeleton is repulsed. If Artus had been unlucky enough to roll a total of 16, the spell would have had no effect. It is then likely the skeleton would be close enough to force Artus to fight him (see combat).

CLERICAL SPELLS AVAILABLE TO ALYNN

Augury: Tells if the act considered will have a good or ill effect on the cleric.

Cure Disease: Completely cures any disease immediately.

Heal Wounds: Restores 1 D6 of hit points lost.

Detect Evil: Causes all evil men and creatures within sight of the cleric to glow with a green light.

Find Traps: Causes all traps within sight of the cleric to glow pale yellow.

Light: Fills any room with bright white light. This causes undead to attack at −2 (subtract 2 from their

INTRODUCTION

total roll in combat). The light will last until the cleric leaves the room or is killed.

Sanctuary: Protects the cleric from all physical attacks; the cleric himself may not attack or capture anything while the spell lasts. This spell lasts only a limited time even though, as a cleric of Cearn, Alynn is particularly well protected. Patient opponents may simply wait it out.

Silence: Prevents all sound from occurring in the immediate area around the cleric.

Speak with Animals: Lets the cleric converse with any one animal chosen. It does not make the animal smarter or friendlier. A hungry lion is more likely to tell you he is about to eat you than to discuss philosophy.

Spirit Hammer: Attacks any opponent twice for 1 D6.

Turn Undead: Forces any undead near the cleric to be driven away.

Remember, you can use each spell only once. Be sure to mark the spells off your record sheet when you use them.

RECORD SHEET

ALYNN, CLERIC OF CEARN

Strength 11
Intelligence 13
Wisdom............... 15
Constitution 13
Dexterity 12
Charisma 10

Skill Level 0

Hit Points:............ 15

Magical Items:
1.
2
3.
4.
5.

Items Carried: mace, chain-mail armor, food, and holy symbol (double ankh).

Spells Chosen:

To begin *Quest for the Demon Gate,* turn to the Prologue.

SWORDQUEST

Quest for the
DEMON GATE

Prologue

Rotting flesh walking over soft earth cannot be heard more than a few feet away. Nothing living hears the approach of the soft, even footsteps, and those that are not alive do not care.

To the nervous monk, the darkness poses a nameless threat. He raises his lantern a little higher, its wan yellow light barely illuminating the blackness. A few steps away, in the stygian shadows beneath the abbey's wall, something waits. It likes night, when the inky blackness echoes its own emptiness. Darkness flows through it and fills the gaps left by a long-absent soul. Perhaps it is not even aware that it exists, this moldering remnant of a warrior long dead.

Above, the monk walks his rounds along the stone-and-mortar wall. He is beyond fear. Terror and exhaustion have settled inside him, and from them has grown a numbness, the kind that is beyond despair and may lead to unexpected courage. Sometimes, but not in this elderly cleric. Eyes that have seen too much now see too little. The beat of his own heart pounds in his head while the noise of bone jutting through decayed flesh scraping against the wall goes unheard. With no other sound, the creature pulls itself up and strikes.

As a rusting blade grates between his ribs, the pain shocks the cleric into awareness for his last instant of life. Without a sound he falls, now a potential recruit for the enemy he has been guarding against. Shapes, black in the unnatural night, swarm over the unguarded wall.

Section 1

1

Alynn is cursing Orlow and whoever made the decision to leave the Ankh in the abbey. "Was it not enough they maintained the last refuge before the Mistwall?" he asks. "Was it not enough they faced constant attack by those followers of the Darklord?"

As expected, he receives no answer. Years ago he had given up waiting for answers. For longer than he cares to remember, Alynn has marked time. A warrior tired of battle, he found a sort of refuge in this outpost of Cearn, the patron of Sanctuary and Shelter. He is aware the others knew of his lack of faith, but tolerated him simply because he was part of the place. Of nearly a hundred brothers only the high priest and two others have been here longer.

Alynn does not look old, nor is he yet forty summers into this reincarnation. The acolytes of Cearn tend to arrive under questionable circumstances and stay only until the drudgery becomes unbearable. Many who stayed had been, like Alynn, men who once lived by the sword. Their training as warriors was more than necessary for survival this close to the Mistwall. Never before had the Darklord concentrated such a large force against the unimportant abbey. Alynn is reminded of the cause of the siege, an Ankh, the ancient symbol of the powers of light.

Three days earlier, Orlow the Wizard and a small band of companions emerged from the Mistwall. With them they carried a golden Ankh. In the talisman's center a ruby throbbed with light of its own.

The ruby, the elderly Wizard had explained, was both a barrier and a gateway. A Demon Gate that opened into the realm of Demons and a barrier that kept the demons from this plane. Once before, the Darklord had summoned a powerful demon through it. Only by the heroism of a lowly guardsman had the demon been banished. Auguries now warned the Demon Gate would again be opened when the moon was dark.

Orlow and his companions had ventured into the

Section 1

Darklord's lands. They emerged fewer in number, but still with the Ankh. When a crisis in Terverni summoned the Wizard away, he left the Ankh behind in the abbey.

There was no light the next dawn. Instead of the sun rising, the skies grew darker. Those few who ventured beyond the abbey's walls had not returned. A large party sent out to find them encountered only their gnawed bones. The first attack on the abbey had been made at midnight by the hour candles, though the sky was no darker or more sullen than it had been at noon. The attackers moved with inhuman silence, flesh dropping from yellowed bone. Three days passed, bringing two more midnight attacks, since the darkness had come. A score of brothers were dead or too badly wounded to defend the abbey's walls.

By the hour candle it is dawn, so Alynn rouses himself to begin his chores. Most of the brothers remain asleep, assuming regularity in the attacks of the undead and exhausted from the constant tension.

As he crosses the courtyard, the blond cleric finds new annoyance in the heavy mace hanging from the cord at his waist. Waiting for a bucket to fill with water, he studies his own reflection in the well a few feet below. Slight of build and fair, he looks younger than his years. The strain of the siege shows in dark patches below his blue eyes. Alynn has just pulled the bucket from the well when he hears the warning.

"Behind you!" a woman's voice yells. He spins to confront his attacker.

The zombie stands a head taller than he, clad in rusting armor. A spear, the shaft half hidden by moss, is clutched in a hand that shows more bone than flesh. The odor of decay fills the sullen air. Glancing around nervously, Alynn can see no sign of the woman who has warned him. Then the abomination jabs at him with surprising speed.

ZOMBIE
To Hit Alynn: 13   To Be Hit: 10   Hit Points: 5
Damage with Spear: 1 D6

Section 2

If Alynn defeats the zombie, turn to section 2.
If the zombie wins, turn to section 3.

2

The zombie moves with cautious ease, using the greater reach of its spear to full advantage. Alynn realizes he would have stood no chance against the skilled warrior whose shadow now serves the Darklord. He tries to take advantage of the creature's slower reflexes and decaying strength to dart in and strike a disabling blow, but the spearpoint always seems to block his way. Slowly, the living man is forced back. Finally he finds his calves pressed against the low wall of the well.

Another lunge of the spear and the point tangles in the cleric's robe, nearly pushing him into the open well. A wild swing of his mace forces the zombie back. Alynn swings again, aiming to smash a hand, only to discover the hand gone and the spear once again driving toward his ribs. His loose cassock again tangles the spearpoint, giving the cleric the fraction of a second he needs to dodge the fatal blow.

"Hit it low!" the same woman's voice urges. Alynn risks a glance at the zombie's legs. The flesh over the left leg is nearly gone, rotted away perhaps from the wound that brought death. Only the brittle bone remains between tatters of black, putrescent muscle.

Ducking below a spearthrust Alynn swings his mace low and parallel to the ground. He is rewarded with a satisfying crack. The brittle bones splinter, and the creature topples forward. Lurching to one side, Alynn readies himself to face another attack by the crippled monster. To his surprise the zombie lies sprawled, unmoving.

"When you break their integrity, they perish," the voice came again. "Hurry to the altar!"

"Thanks," Alynn yelled over his shoulder, dashing toward the darkened chapel. No one stood there to answer, though he would have sworn the voice came from only a few feet away.

Section 3

The chapel is lit by a few torches and candles on the altar. Outside, Alynn can hear the sounds of men dying. The stench of decay is less oppressive in this holy place, though still present. Glittering on the altar are three items: the Ankh, the mace of the high priest, and a scroll in a silver case. Moving toward the altar, Alynn glimpses movement in the doorway leading to the cloisters. Hoping to see one of the brothers, he turns and begins a greeting.

The word dies in his throat when he sees the bony hand of a skeleton. Painfully the cleric realizes most of his brothers were asleep in the cloisters. If a skeleton has passed through, few can remain to fight. An even more fearsome darkness fills the doorway behind the skeletal warrior. A darkness that seems to move and flow along the walls.

His heart beating quickly and his breath coming in gasps, Alynn races to the altar. For a second he glances at the threatening shadow and then grabs the Ankh. He must prevent the Darklord from seizing it. Only two days remain until the dark of the moon. The unnatural darkness and the skeleton race toward him. The cleric hesitates for a second longer and reaches out again.

If Alynn should take the mace, turn to section 10.

If Alynn should take the scroll, turn to section 7.

3

The first blow by the zombie nearly skewers Alynn. The spearpoint rakes his side, and he feels a warmth trickle down his hip. The zombie moves with cautious ease, using the greater reach of its spear to full advantage. Alynn realizes he would have stood no chance against the skilled warrior whose empty husk he now faces. The cleric tries to take advantage of the creature's slower reflexes and decaying strength to dart in and strike a disabling blow. Whenever he tries to strike, the spear keeps him at bay. Slowly, the living man is forced back. Finally his calves press against the low wall of the well.

Another lunge of the spear and the point tangles in

Section 4

the cleric's robe, nearly pushing him into the open well. A wild swing of his mace forces the zombie back. Alynn swings again, aiming to smash a hand, only to discover the hand gone and the spear thrusting toward his midriff.

"No!" the woman's voice rises to almost painful intensity, but the warning is too late.

Automatically the cleric throws himself backward. His feet are stopped unexpectedly by the edge of the well. Alynn flails his arms to keep his balance. The point of the spear reaches the struggling cleric's chest, and the force of the blow drives him further off balance. He has a brief glimpse of the dark sky, and then the world erupts into bright colors. Darkness follows as Alynn tumbles into the well and strikes his head against its stone wall.

Turn to section 13.

4

The whole situation is becoming too much for Alynn to accept. It is almost as if he is living a nightmare and none of it seems quite real. His memories of working in the gardens or tending the livestock seem more real than the devastation around him. Taking the armor off the weeks old corpse is a gruesome task which seems only appropriate in this horrible dreamland.

The chain itself is covered with rust and stained by the decaying body beneath it. When Alynn begins to unbuckle the straps, he gags at the odor of putrefying flesh. His skin seems to crawl where it brushes against a milky white ooze which has seeped through the chain's links. He fights the urge to scrape it through the dusty ground and forces himself to continue. Twice he nearly abandons the task, only to be urged back by Rhea. Finally all the rusty buckles are loosened and he pulls the armor free.

Maggots stream from a deep wound in the long dead warrior's chest. The cleric recoils in disgust, nearly tripping over the much newer corpse on the ground behind him. He stares at the recently fallen form of a

Section 4

novice, its face frozen in a look of terror. Just a few days earlier the youth had stayed up all night to help the birthing of a new colt. Alynn wonders if the abbey's animals have been slaughtered as well. Then a deep spring of anger and hatred bursts open somewhere deep inside the grieving human. Alynn is frightened by the churning red hate as it flows through him. Anger at the Darklord. For years he has been taught to suppress such "evil" emotions. Still, the anger feels right and somehow makes everything a little more bearable.

With renewed determination, Alynn strides purposefully to the fallen borderer and bends over the corpse. With rapid, decisive motions he continues removing the enchanted chain mail. The cleric nearly can't continue when one arm, barely attached by a few dried ligaments, pulls free along with the coat. By the time he has extracted the remnants of the arm, he is himself covered in gore. Looking down at himself the man wonders why he is no longer as offended by the stench of death which is beginning to fill the courtyard as the day warms and sunlight hurries the process of decomposition.

"There is time for you to wash the chain and yourself," Rhea suggests tactfully.

Alynn goes first to the well from which he had recently emerged. Looking into it, he sees the water's surface is covered by a layer of scum. Below that surface, in the no longer clear water, the cleric can see the vague form of a zombie. Washing in that water is unlikely to make him more appealing.

"There is one source of clean water left," Rhea reminds the man. "In the Blessing font."

It takes the numbed cleric several seconds to react to her observation. Then he feels the beginnings of indignation. His anger is willing to strike out at anything connected with the disaster.

"That is blessed water!" he protests.

"And you are on a holy mission," Rhea counters. "I doubt Cearn will be upset with your using holy water, considering the entire temple has just been destroyed."

Looking around him, Alynn suddenly feels drained,

Section 5

he only wants to be done and away. The abbey he had known and been sheltered in for years has simply ceased to be. Trying not to think about how he may well be being tricked into desecrating his own holy water font, Alynn enters the chapel and hurriedly strips away his garments. Using a silver vessel, he pours cups of the sacred water over himself. Then he rinses off the chain-mail coat and his own clothes in the waist-deep stone font. Through a low window Alynn can see the sprawled form of the High Priest. His chest appears to have been burst from inside, leaving a crater lined with jagged bone and torn muscle. Anxious to be away, the man puts on his still wet clothes and pulls the enchanted chain mail over them.

Include +1 armor on Alynn's list of magical items. In all future combats subtract 1 from any attacker's total when determining if the cleric is hit.

Turn to section 5.

5

The Mistwall, thought to be an air elemental bound by the Darklord's geas, has marked the border of the Darklord's domain for two generations. Over the decades it has advanced, sometimes slowly, sometimes in dramatic leaps. Never has it retreated. More than anything else, it is a symbol of the ominous power of the dark Wizard.

Alynn hesitates before entering the swirling darkness. Now, at night, the Mistwall flickers like a will-o'-the-wisp. The colors change subtly from sickly green to pale purple, mutating before the cleric can identify any one color or shape. Nerves racked by his exposure to the undead at the abbey, he perceives the Mistwall as threateningly alive. Rhea, who has been silent for long hours as he walked northward, senses his fear.

"The Mistwall is harmless in itself."

Alynn listens intently, trying to catch any note of familiarity in the voice. If it is merely a sign of his own insanity, it should be a voice from his past. During the long trek there has been little to distract him from

Section 5

dwelling on the slaughter he left behind. Speculating on Rhea and doubting his own sanity have offered a pleasant haven in contrast. In a way, he is relieved to hear her speak again, glad for the company in this forsaken place, even if it is only a hallucination.

"What can you do to help me?" the cleric inquires, anxious to get a better understanding of the nature of his companion before continuing. Nor, a core of honesty requires him to admit to himself, is he anxious to plunge into the swirling mist a few steps ahead.

"By being myself," she answers cryptically.

"But what are you?"

"What you don't see. Now you must hurry! The abandoned temple is east of here, a four-, maybe five-hour walk. The Ankh is there already."

"How can you know this?" Alynn demands.

He waits dozens of heartbeats for the answer. None comes.

"Answer me," he demands.

Still only silence.

Finally, though seething with frustration, the follower of Cearn plunges into the mists. For hours he walks in silence. The wall is a confusion of vaguely colored clouds. Each colored wisp moves in its own direction, seemingly unaware they should be static in the moist stagnant air. As Alynn passes through the first finger of cloud, this one a sickly pale purple, the muscles on his back tense.

The cloud's touch is so soft, Alynn is at first barely aware of it. By the fourth passage, the cleric discovers his skin is covered with a clammy dampness. It is not attar and not really oil, but something in between. Ominously he notices the gap between the streaks of mist are getting smaller. Either the Mistwall gets thicker or it is becoming aware of his presence. If it is aware, then likely the Darklord has also learned of his passage through it. Soon the mists are so thick the cleric can do nothing but worry and concentrate on walking in a straight line.

"A little to the left," Rhea's voice is conversational, as if there had been no gap in the discussion. Alynn bites off a reply and veers to his left. He doubts he can

Section 5

find his way back out of the ever shifting Mistwall. Like it or not, he is committed and, without some sort of help, his mission is doomed.

He hears the sounds of the struggle before anything is visible. At first it is a faint snarl. Then more clearly he hears the thunk of steel on flesh.

"Don't. It's not your concern," Rhea admonishes, but Alynn rushes toward the sound. He sees a dark-haired woman to his left, less than twenty feet away.

The woman is tall, nearly his height. She wears a plain gown nearly as black as her hair. In her right hand she holds a curved dagger, which she is wielding to keep two manlike creatures at bay. The woman glimpses Alynn from the corner of her eye and half spins, thinking him a new menace. One of the creatures takes advantage of the distraction to rake the woman's dagger arm with clawlike nails. Backing toward him the woman silently pleads for the cleric's assistance.

"Don't!" Rhea warns again.

Alynn is already in motion, placing himself between the woman and her attackers. For the first time he gets a clear look at them.

They are Orcs—squat, barely humanoid, with thick ridges of bone over their eyes. Their hair is unkempt and dark, their skin a listless gray. Their armor is tattered leather, torn and in poor repair, and each hefts a thick club. One grunts as it perceives the intruder. The two creatures begin to move apart.

If Alynn should use a Turn Undead spell, turn to section 14.

If Alynn should use a Spirit Hammer spell, turn to section 6.

If Alynn should do combat with the woman's attackers, turn to section 19.

If Alynn should use a Sanctuary spell, turn to section 11.

Section 6, 7

6

Roll 3 D6.

If the total is 16 or less, continue reading.

If the total is greater than 16, turn to section 19.

Alynn finds it surprisingly hard to concentrate on the Spirit Hammer spell while his attackers approach. Nervously he draws a tiny hammer from the pocket of his robe. Chanting slowly so as not to mispronounce the spell, he summons the power of Cearn to smite the monsters.

Behind him the cleric can hear the harsh breathing of the woman. Backing slowly to prevent her assailants from trapping him between them, Alynn nearly shouts the final word. Then he flings the hammer.

A howl of pain echoes through the eerie mists. Feeling he once more can strike, the cleric concentrates on the same foe. Another scream comes, softer and ending abruptly.

"Behind you!" shouts a familiar voice. Alynn ducks just fast enough to avoid the other monster's club. The rough wood comes so close he can feel the wind of its passage.

"Getting to be a habit," Rhea comments, sounding satisfied with herself.

Cross the Spirit Hammer spell off the record sheet.

Turn to section 19.

Before beginning the combat, roll 2 D6. Subtract the total from the hit points of one of the Orcs. If the total is greater than the 6 hit points each Orc has, the first has been slain by the Spirit Hammer spell. Only the second will then have to be fought.

7

The scroll case is sealed with wax. On the seal is the sign for Heal Wounds. Alynn prays the priest who created the scroll completed the enchantment. The

Section 8

scrape of a skeletal foot across the chapel floor then rivets his attention.

"Go! Now!" the woman's voice commands. Alynn rushes toward his skeletal enemy, his mace banging painfully against his leg. Out of the corner of his eye the cleric can see the shadow drift toward him, a mass of blackness in the weak light of the flickering torches and candles. Acting out of desperation rather than courage, he swings his mace at the skeleton.

Bones shatter even as the enemy swings its weapon. The skeleton's staff glances against the side of Alynn's head, causing the room to darken and forcing him to clutch a pillar for support. The cleric stumbles out the door, half conscious, driven by fear of the shadow behind him.

As he emerges from the chapel, a hand grasps the Ankh. Through blurry eyes Alynn sees the face of Pieter, a fellow priest and friend. He relaxes his grip. But when his eyes clear, he sees rotting flesh. He realizes Pieter has been missing for three days. Before he can react, the talisman is wrenched from his grasp.

Awkwardly Alynn tries to raise his mace and strike a blow at the corpse of his friend. Before he can complete the action, a vicious blow lands in the center of his back.

Unexpected pain robs every muscle of its strength. The cleric feels himself stumble forward from the force of the blow. His muddled thoughts are more concerned with the terrible cold of his attacker's touch than his progress across the courtyard.

He is half unconscious when he stumbles over the low stones that mark the edge of the well.

Add a scroll containing one Heal Wounds spell to Alynn's list of magical items.

Turn to section 13.

8

A few inches in front of Alynn's face the wall dances. As the cleric begins to fall, he finds the burnt skin on his arms has tightened so as to make it impossible to

Section 9, 10

bend his elbows more than a few inches. The wall looms ahead and then falls away as he bounces painfully off of it.

He tries to look past the glowing altar at Lyla, but a throbbing redness blocks his vision. He tries to call out to her, but only a barely audible croak escapes his parched throat before it closes completely. As the dying cleric feebly raises a hand in the hope of invoking a cure on himself, oblivion ends his torment.

Turn to section 29.

9

The exertion of climbing seems to warm the cleric. The shivering subsides, and some color returns to his fingers. A cut on his ribs reopens, sending a slender trickle of warm blood down his side. Alynn has nearly reached the top when his foot slips off a moss-covered rock.

For a few seconds he hangs suspended by the grip of his hands on the damp rock wall. Then his numb fingers refuse further abuse. The last sound Alynn hears as he scrapes painfully down the side of the well is a woman's laughter.

Anger erupts as he clears the surface of the water. An anger spurred by the pain of scraped ribs and arms stung by the water. With sullen determination the cleric draws himself once more up the wall, this time choosing each foot- and handhold more carefully. Less than a minute later he lies sprawled in the courtyard.

Subtract one point of damage received in the fall from Alynn's hit points.

Turn to section 12.

10

Alynn lifts the sacred mace, wrapping the leather strap around his wrist. Clutching the Ankh in his other hand, he surveys the chapel. The shadow has stopped moving, hovering near the doorway to the cloisters. The skeleton still moves toward the cleric with steady,

Section 11

mindless steps, blocking his exit to the courtyard. As the horror lifts a staff over its skull, its bones grate and grind.

"Go! Now!" the woman's voice commands. Alynn rushes toward his skeletal enemy, his mace banging painfully into his leg. Out of the corner of his eye the cleric can see the shadow drift toward him, a mass of blackness in the weak light of the flickering torches and candles. Acting out of desperation rather than courage, he swings the sacred mace at the skeleton.

Bones shatter even as yellowed arms bring the raised staff down. The skeleton's weapon glances off the side of Alynn's head, causing the room to darken and forcing him to clutch a pillar for support. The cleric stumbles out the door, half conscious, driven by fear of the unknown darkness that pursues him.

As he emerges from the chapel, a hand grasps the Ankh. Through blurry eyes Alynn sees the face of Pieter, a fellow priest and friend. He relaxes his grip. But as his thoughts clear he realizes Pieter has been missing for three days. The talisman is violently wrenched from his grasp by gray and rotting hands that had been his friend's.

Awkwardly Alynn tries to raise the sacred mace and strike a blow at the undead cleric. His arms seem heavy and distant. But before he can complete the action, a vicious blow lands in the center of his back.

Unexpected pain robs his every muscle of strength. The cleric feels himself stumbling forward, more concerned with the terrible cold of his attacker's touch than his progress across the courtyard.

He is close to unconscious when he stumbles over the low stones that mark the edge of the well.

Add a +2 mace to Alynn's list of magical items. (He may use this in future combats.)

Turn to section 13.

11

Roll 3 D6.

If the total is 16 or less, continue reading.

Section 12

If the total is greater than 16, turn to section 19.

The creatures' grunts grow louder as they circle him. Alynn watches, carefully chanting the Sanctuary spell and wishing the formula were shorter. The nearer monster raises his club to strike just as the invocation ends.

A soft yellow luminescence, barely visible in the shifting mists, shelters the cleric. Already Alynn feels the warmth and comfort of the protective field. The Orc brings down his club, and the knobby wood bounces away harmlessly, inches from the head of the cleric, who is now smiling.

A scream of frustration fills the air. Both of the misshapen creatures retreat, their worried grunting growing louder as they approach each other. Then there is silence. Alynn is dismayed to see the creatures begin to move around him, one on each side. Glancing behind, he sees the dark-haired woman tearing a strip of cloth from her gown to bind her injured arm.

The follower of Cearn realizes that while he is protected by the Sanctuary spell, the woman isn't. For a moment he hesitates, knowing that to move or attack will negate his own safety. Then the creatures rush by him, one on either side. He acts.

If Alynn should use his Turn Undead spell, turn to section 14.

If Alynn should use his Spirit Hammer spell, turn to section 6.

If Alynn should attack with his mace, turn to section 19.

12

Lying on his back, the first thing Alynn notices is that the sun is low in the sky. Many hours have passed, if this is the same day the battle began. Rolling onto his side he surveys the courtyard.

Sprawled awkwardly nearby is the body of Jlenklen. He and Allyn had shared cleaning duty just the week before. Jlenklen's head lies at an impossible angle, and flies have already gathered over the corpse. Looking

Section 12

beyond it, Alynn sees the devastation that remains of the Lesser Abbey of Cearn the Protector.

The bodies of several other clerics lie contorted on the gray stones. Among them are a few bodies clad in rusted armor and far into the process of decay. Attempting to stand, Alynn has to kick aside human bones.

Cearn has given much protection, he thinks bitterly. He barely recognizes the faces of men he has known for years.

"I wouldn't insult any god too freely," the woman's voice remonstrates. "You are going to need all the help you can get—soon."

Alynn begins to mouth an angry retort and then realizes he has not spoken. Even his thoughts are not hidden from the mysterious voice.

"What are you?" he asks instead.

"It would be best if you just accept that I am," the answer comes smoothly. "Accept that I will help you."

"Help me?"

"To recover the Ankh," the voice answered matter-of-factly. "And it is high time to begin."

Nervously Alynn enters the burnt-out chapel. Its altar is empty and scorched. For a moment he hesitates, then kneels to make a plea to Cearn for spells. The peace he sometimes finds in prayer does not come. With a sigh he rises.

Choose the spells Alynn will have and note them on the record sheet. See pages 20 and 21 of the introduction for what spells are available.

Completing his petition Alynn continues into the cloister. More bodies greet him, those of men he had known mixed with the even grislier remains of their attackers. The cleric changes into a dry robe, and is relieved when his shivering stops.

"I don't remember volunteering to recover the Ankh," the cleric comments sharply to the empty air, his pride stung. "Nor am I eager to do so because a nameless voice tells me to."

"A name?" The voice sounds amused and it jars Alynn. "You can call me Rhea, if a name is so important to you.... Yes, Rhea has a nice sound to it."

Section 12

"How can one man hope to recover the Ankh when so many could not defend it?" Alynn questions, surveying the remains of his comrades. "How can I succeed when so many holier than I could not?"

"Unless you wish all the citizens of the Empire to suffer the same fate as these, you have no choice."

The bodies of his friends offer a persuasive argument. Nor can he see any reason to stay. The quiet solitude of the abbey is gone forever. Euphoria at having survived where so many had perished sets in.

"I will do it!" Alynn declares to the seemingly empty room, sounding pompous even to himself.

Rhea's comment is a tinkle of laughter.

"It is not hopeless, you know," she explains. "It took much energy to animate so many creatures. The Darklord will be drained. He will need to rest until the last moment if he is to open another gateway.

"In the meantime the Ankh is still close by, hidden in the ruins of a temple just beyond the Mistwall. If he is to regain his strength, the Darklord can set only a few guards upon it."

For a moment the task sounds possible. Feeling the need to do something but still reluctant to venture forth, he kneels by the nearest fallen cleric and begins the ritual of departure.

"No time for that!" the voice remonstrates curtly. "There are too many of them and they won't care."

Alynn looks up, offended, then realizes once more there is nothing to see.

"If you don't want to have thousands to pray for, it is time to go. Something you will need lies in the courtyard by the well."

Annoyed and frustrated, the cleric rouses himself from the familiar ritual of prayer. The woman's irreverence causes him once again to wonder what she could be. He has only her—no, its—word that it is concerned about saving the Empire. Just as easily it could be tricking him into some evil action for its own purposes. Rhea certainly is neither reverent nor respectful. It might even have been left behind by the Darklord to take care of any survivors such as himself. He resolves to be on his guard.

Section 13

* * *

As they enter the courtyard, Rhea directs Alynn to a portion of the wall. Fallen there are the long dead remains of a Telandor borderer. His flesh is black and swollen with decay.

"Take the chain mail," she instructs.

Alynn notices the man's armor is in better condition than any on the remains of the other attackers. On close examination he sees that it is filthy, but it has no rust.

"You will need protection," Rhea urges.

The cleric wonders if this is a trap. Will this armor slay him as it did the borderer? Could it turn him into a soulless undead? Looking about, he can see another fallen soldier, less decayed. Alynn wonders if he should take his armor instead.

If Alynn should take the Telandor borderer's armor, turn to section 4.

If Alynn should take the soldier's armor, turn to section 15.

13

"Wake up!" the voice persists. "Alynn, wake up!"

The cleric comes awake with an awareness of cold, cold so penetrating it is painful. He remembers the touch of the shadow's hand, and his pulse races.

The rapid beating of his heart brings him awake with an abrupt surge of agony. He is cold. Cold and mystifyingly damp. His head hurts, his back aches, everything screams its own special message of pain. Reluctantly he opens an eye to find himself looking at the reflection of clear blue skies on glistening water. As his focus improves, the rough stone sides of the wall come into focus.

Under his chest is a beam over which he is draped. His arms and legs dangle in the cold water. Pulling himself up, the cleric is surprised to find the mace still strapped to his wrist.

"You have to leave now," the woman's voice urges, "or it will be too late."

Alynn starts at the voice, certain that he is alone in

Section 14

the well. Carefully he searches the opening eight feet above for some sign of the speaker.

"Where are you?" he croaks.

"You can't see me," is the disconcerting reply. The voice sounds only inches away.

"What are you?" the cleric asks, his pulse once again racing as memories of the night's attackers return. Then he remembers the unexplainable warnings.

"You helped me," Alynn comments hesitantly.

"You weren't doing so well."

"Why did you help me?"

"You were closest to the Ankh," the woman's voice explains unsympathetically.

"Where are you?" the cleric presses.

"Nearby, always nearby," it answers cryptically.

"What are you?" Alynn demands again, though his voice breaks as a wave of shivering seizes him.

"You had better climb out of the well while you have the strength," the woman's voice evades.

Still shivering, Alynn grasps the wall nearby. He has climbed the wall once before, to retrieve a bucket when its rope worked loose. With his first effort, the cleric realizes just how badly his body has already been abused.

Roll 3 D6.

If the total rolled is the same as or lower than Alynn's value for Dexterity, turn to section 12.

If the total rolled is greater than Alynn's Dexterity value, turn to section 9.

14

Roll 3 D6.

If the total is 16 or less, continue reading.

If the total is greater than 16, turn to section 19.

Drawing himself up to face both attackers, Alynn begins to chant the Turn Undead spell. With his free hand he gestures in the air between them. A sign appears, which Alynn knows will drive back all but the most powerful undead.

With a snuffling sound, the nearer of the two attackers walks through the glowing sign and swings his club at the astonished cleric.

Cross the Turn Undead spell off Alynn's record sheet. Then turn to section 19. The monsters now have the first attack.

15

"The other armor was better," the voice admonishes, "but so be it."

Alynn cannot hear any anger or frustration in Rhea's tone.

Alynn is now wearing a functional, if not appealing, suit of chain mail.

Turn to section 5.

16

"Thank you," the dark-haired woman says in a low voice. She is young and quite beautiful, with long dark hair and large brown eyes. Her black gown, drenched with sweat, clings most pleasantly, showing a lean but full figure.

"Are you hurt?" he asks, feeling suddenly tongue-tied. There were few women at the Lesser Abbey of Cearn, and those the wives of other priests.

"You'll be sorry," Rhea's voice taunts.

"I doubt it," Alynn snaps back.

By the rescued woman's mystified look, it is obvious that she doesn't hear Rhea. For a long second Alynn again wonders if he has gone insane. Is he hearing a voice that isn't there? Is he possessed by some demon?

"Doubt what?" the young woman asks, confused.

"Stupid sometimes, insane no," that same voice answers.

"I doubt anything could mar such beauty," he ad-libs to the woman he has saved. Not bad, he decides, for an improvised comment.

Section 16

"Trite," a familiar voice echoes in his head.

"I think I'm all right," the wounded woman answers. "I am Lyla."

"What are you doing on this side of the Mistwall?"

"I'm a Gama trader. My people were attacked. I was knocked unconscious. When I came to, three Orcs were carrying me through the mist."

"Three?"

"The other's body should be a few hundred paces that way," Lyla explains, gesturing vaguely. As if reminded, she walks over to pick up the curved dagger. With a smooth gesture she hides the blade in the folds of her gown. Even watching closely, Alynn isn't sure where it has gone. Smiling, the woman turns to him.

"I am grateful for your help. Why would a priest of Cearn venture through the Mistwall?"

Seeing no reason to lie, the cleric tells her the story of the Ankh and his quest to regain it. The woman seems sympathetic, even impressed by his mission. To his own surprise, Alynn finds he appreciates her admiration. Despite the surroundings and his desperate journey, the cleric is almost enjoying himself.

"You can't get back to your people alone," Alynn observes. "Why don't you..."

"Don't do it," Rhea's voice interrupts.

"...join me on the quest?" he finishes rebelliously. The voice's superior attitude inspires the invitation as much as his desire to keep Lyla safe. It seems right to take her with him, and he resents the voice's coldheartedness. Carefully, he resists speculating on any other desires Lyla is inspiring.

"You're making this harder," the voice in his head warns.

Alynn chokes back a retort, concentrating instead on the beauty beside him. Once invited, she readily joins him on the quest. He stands amazed as she searches the corpses of the fallen Orcs and smiles at the few silver pieces she finds. Rhea is silent as they walk, but Lyla proves to be excellent company.

She asks the lonely cleric questions about himself and his life as a priest of Cearn. To Alynn's delight, even his mildest witticisms seem to amuse her greatly,

Section 16

and his dull existence interests her without limit. Lyla's habit of clutching his arm as they walk over the grassy steppes produces a most pleasant sensation. He occasionally wants to say something romantic, but whenever the time seems right she dances away or distracts him with some comment.

They walk for some time until the swirling mists start to clear. Overhead the stars are once more visible. Alynn feels tension, of which he has not even been aware, melt away.

"We are less than a day from the abbey," Lyla says, grasping his arm. "I'm very tired."

Alynn is also exhausted from the strain of the last day, stumbling over the rough ground, eyelids sagging over burning eyes. Sleep sounds most appealing.

"There may not be time. You have more important things to do than cuddle some wench you've just met," Rhea warns.

Alynn ignores the warning. He is so tired he barely has the energy to feel a twinge of resentment. The cleric allows Lyla to lead him to a sheltered area between two boulders.

"Only until dawn," the phantom voice warns, but he is too tired to care. With a sigh, Alynn and Lyla settle down against a boulder. Lyla, to his delight, lays her head against his shoulder. Instinctively, Alynn wraps his arm around her. For a brief instant he enjoys the beautiful woman's closeness. Then exhaustion triumphs, and he falls into a dreamless sleep.

"Alynn! Alynn, wake up!"

The voice echoes from a great distance. Reluctantly, the cleric pulls himself from the soft pool of slumber. To his dismay, the sun has risen far above the horizon. Confused, he starts to stand, only to stop at the unfamiliar weight against his side.

He glances down at Lyla. She looks as beautiful in the daylight as she did under the stars. Then all the other memories of the last days surge back to him. The reality of the loss of his companions and friends at the abbey washes over him. The hopelessness of his quest overwhelms him.

Section 16

"Get it going, you slug," a woman's voice grates inside his skull. "Going to stay asleep until some demon wakes you up?"

Alynn starts to shake his head to deny the accusation. The stabbing pain in his temples reminds the cleric of the abuse and tension he has endured. Stifling a groan, he rubs his forehead. The movement disturbs Lyla. With almost feline grace she stretches. Alynn allows himself the pleasure of being distracted by her shape as the robe pulls taut. Seeing his glance, Lyla smiles in a friendly manner, but says nothing.

"We had better go," she says, still smiling.

"You had better get going," Rhea's voice insists almost simultaneously.

With a careful laugh the cleric lifts himself against the boulder and strides into the open steppeland. It is a sunny day, nearly cloudless. After the darkness of the siege, Alynn finds the sunlight delightful. For a few seconds he is content to absorb its warmth. The quest seems a distant thing, surely involving someone else, not a quiet and very average cleric of Cearn.

As he turns to face Lyla, his spirits sag when he sees the Mistwall behind them. The writhing cloud of gray and bilious green moves in ways no wind could inspire. With a sinking sensation he contemplates this visible sign of the power of the man he is venturing to defeat.

"What makes you think he's a man?" Rhea asks disconcertingly. "Or even human?"

"Can't you stay out of my mind?" Alynn asks angrily. Embarrassed, he remembers other thoughts inspired by Lyla's beauty and friendly nature during the night's walk.

"No," Rhea answers simply.

"Well, where do we go from here?" he asks silently.

"Straight ahead until you reach a canyon, then left, straight into it."

"What's there?"

"The Ankh."

Misunderstanding Alynn's silent concentration, Lyla comments, "When you're done praying to Cearn, we had best get moving."

Embarrassed, Alynn becomes aware he has neither

Section 17, 18

asked the deity for spells nor even offered the barest of worship. Hoping Cearn will understand if he prays while walking, he starts in the direction Rhea indicated. Lyla follows without comment.

At this point you may choose three new spells. Once you have chosen them, list them on your record sheet. Wipe out the ones from the previous day. Only these three new spells may be attempted.

Turn to section 23.

17

Alynn's mind races. Undead fear strong light. Hurriedly he recites the words to summon the brightness of the Light spell. More than once he has heard an undead in the light is nearly helpless.

With a whoosh of breath, the cleric finishes the short incantation. Around him the daylight glows more brightly. Frustrated, Alynn notices the difference is not great. The late morning sun is already nearly as bright as the light any spell can conjure.

The nearer monster is close enough for the scraps of flesh on its bones to be disgustingly visible.

Turn to section 30.

18

Alynn recites the last words of the Spirit Hammer spell just as the hammer comes free of his pocket. With an underhand toss, he throws it at the approaching monster. The creature shudders from the magical impact. The long-dead harpy is close now, close enough for the scraps of flesh on its bones to be disgustingly visible. Concentrating once more, Alynn commands the Spirit Hammer to strike again. Shards of bone trail behind the silent attacker.

Roll 2 D6.

If the total rolled is greater than 7, Alynn has to fight only one skeletal harpy.

Section 19,20

If the total is 7 or less, subtract it from the hit points of the first harpy. The second harpy will join the melee beginning with the second round.

Turn to section 30.

19

ORCS
To Hit Alynn: 12   To Be Hit: 12   Hit Points: 6
Damage with Clubs: 1 D6

If Alynn wins the combat, turn to section 16.

If Alynn is killed, turn to section 29.

20

Lyla must be badly hurt, Alynn decides. Holding the mace ahead of him, he walks toward the fallen woman. As he nears her, the cleric begins to chant the Heal Wounds spell. Warily he watches the wraith as it gathers itself together for another attack.

To heal Lyla the cleric knows he must bend and touch her. The misty form is drifting slowly toward her as well. Nervously Alynn hurries the last few steps and kneels. Even as he completes the chant and puts a healing hand on the woman, the creature surges at him. Alynn watches, struggling to rise in the few instants before it will reach him.

The creature oozes—the cleric can find no other word—toward him. Inside its nebulous form, clouds roil. He is reminded of the Mistwall. The wisps are driven to frenzied movement as the wraith gathers its powers to attack.

Turn to section 28, but give the wraith the first attack.

The Heal Wounds spell has no effect on Lyla. Cross it off your record sheet.

Section 21, 22

21

As the harpy drops toward him, Alynn begins to chant the Turn Undead spell. Speaking quickly, he recites the words that will summon the might of Cearn. From the back of his mind comes a memory of his hurried petition made an hour earlier while distracted by Lyla's beauty and soft voice. Would Cearn deign to grant some of his power to such a negligent follower?

With confidence waning as the harpy swiftly approaches, the cleric stands with arms extended toward the approaching skeletons. When the nearer harpy is close enough for him to see scraps of dried flesh on its bony form, he yells out the final words of the spell.

Roll 3 D6.

If the total is the same as or less than Alynn's value for Wisdom, turn to section 26.

If the total is greater than Alynn's Wisdom value, turn to section 30.

22

Rushing to Lyla, Alynn turns her over. He is relieved to see her chest rise and fall regularly. As he holds her head, her eyes flicker open. She seems unwounded. His own shoulder twinges with pain.

"Forget the girl," Rhea's voice sounds like a distant shout. "You have other troubles."

Looking up, Alynn sees a second form rising over the graveyard. This one also appears to have trouble gathering itself, and then simply waits. After a few endless seconds it beckons Alynn to come to it. Lyla, still on the ground, stares speechless at the second apparition.

If Alynn should hurry into the abbey, turn to section 40.

If Alynn should cast a Turn Undead spell on the apparition, turn to section 31.

Section 23

If Alynn should go to the creature and see what it wants, turn to section 42.

23

Skeletons cast very little shadow. If there had been more than decaying scraps of muscle and tendon over the creatures' bones, Alynn might have been warned of the attack. Instead, his first warning is the tearing pain of sharp fingerbones raking across his shoulder. The force of the blow sends him tumbling into the dried grass.

Landing on his back, the cleric gets his first look at the monsters. The harpy is considered the ugliest of monsters. The head of a woman and the body and jagged claws of a vulture are joined in an unnatural combination. Circling overhead are the skeletons of two of these foul beasts. Their malformed bodies are made hideous and nearly ludicrous by the lack of feathers and flesh.

The claws are real enough. Only the stout chain mail has saved Alynn from a severe wound. Already the shoulder throbs where the torn chain has been driven into his shoulder.

Lyla is cowering behind a small bush some yards away. The woman is staring at the repulsive beasts, trying to keep the scrubbrush between the harpies and herself. Overhead the skeletons defy gravity as well as death, circling higher.

Alynn realizes there is one advantage to his opponents being only the skeletal remains of harpies. No throat remains to wind their enchanted cry. Like the battle in the abbey, this combat will be fought in deathly silence.

The higher harpy dives, its wings suddenly folded close to its skeletal body, blood-tipped claws extend. Its body is a growing blot against the blue sky.

If Alynn should cast a Turn Undead spell, turn to section 21.

If Alynn should cast a Spirit Hammer spell, turn to section 27.

Section 24, 25

If Alynn should cast a Light spell, turn to section 17.

If Alynn should engage the skeletal harpies in combat, turn to section 30.

24

Taking an involuntary step backward, Alynn watches the creature. He keeps his mace raised over one shoulder. Wondering at the nature of his enemy, he mumbles the chant for the Detect Evil spell. Even as the short chant ends, the wraith finishes gathering its form and drifts toward the cleric. Alynn watches, fascinated by the specter as it approaches.

The creature oozes—the cleric can find no other word—toward him. Inside its nebulous form, clouds roil. He is reminded of the Mistwall. The wisps are driven to frenzied movement as the wraith gathers its powers to attack.

Roll 3 D6.

If the total is the same as or less than Alynn's value for Wisdom, turn to section 28.

If the total is greater than Alynn's Wisdom value, turn to section 35 and give the wraith the first attack.

25

"Cearn, I hope you are listening," Alynn says to the clouds. Then he begins to recite the chant for the Spirit Hammer spell. The demon is three times his size. It is hard to read the expression on its lizardlike features, but there is no mistaking the happiness in its eyes. This creature is attacking for the sheer joy of it.

When the spell ends, the cleric lifts his tiny hammer and throws it toward the demon. As it leaves his fingers, the hammer seems to explode in a burst of red light. When his eyes clear, Alynn sees the Spirit Hammer poised above the shocked demon, ready to strike.

The head of the glowing hammer is larger than the demon itself. Snarling, the monster backs slowly away from the enchanted weapon.

Section 26

"Strike," Alynn commands it. With lightning swiftness, the hammer swings down and smacks into the demon. The cleric hears nothing when it hits, but the creature reels. A yellow ichor oozes from a crack in the spider body, and one of its eight spindly legs now hangs useless at its side.

Before the man can order the Spirit Hammer to descend again, a burst of red light appears over the demon. From this light a giant green shield forms. Protected by the magical shield, the demon advances toward its smaller opponent.

Alynn orders the hammer to smash the monster once more, but the blow is stopped by the green shield. In a burst of orange light, both the hammer and the shield disappear. The cleric can feel the empty letdown of failed magic.

Then the demon is hovering a few feet ahead of him, and there is no further chance to use magic. The first time Alynn swings the mace, it passes through the spider's body with no effect. The demon's clawed hand tears a jagged line across the cleric's extended arm, and he reels backward. Then he hears Rhea speak.

"Think about the mace hitting the demon," she says. "This is a place where the thought is as important as the action."

The cleric does as he is told, and his next blow lands with a satisfying impact on the demon's scaly chest.

SPIDER-DEMON
To Hit Alynn: 10   To Be Hit: 11   Hit Points: 6
Damage from Claws: 1 D6

The demon will attack first.

If Alynn defeats the demon, turn to section 124.

If Alynn is killed, turn to section 29.

26

Even in the sunlight the symbol glows reassuringly. Alynn can almost hear the closer skeleton squawk in protest as it flaps its bony wings. Behind it the other long-dead harpy is already winging away.

Section 27, 28

Within minutes both are merely spots in the cloudless sky. Before the symbol has faded, the spots have disappeared. Alynn exhales a deep breath he had not remembered holding.

Turn to section 33.

27

As the harpy drops toward him, Alynn begins to chant the Spirit Hammer spell. Speaking quickly, he recites the words that will summon the might of Cearn. From the back of his mind comes a memory of his hurried petition made an hour earlier while distracted by Lyla's beauty and soft voice. Would Cearn deign to grant power to such a negligent follower?

With confidence waning as the harpy swiftly approaches, the cleric pulls a small hammer from a pocket in his robe. For a nerve-racking second the head catches on the cloth. Glancing upward, Alynn can see the rapidly moving form of the dead harpy. Its claws are tipped with glistening blood—his blood.

Roll 3 D6.

If the total is the same as or less than Alynn's Wisdom value, turn to section 18.

If the total is greater than Alynn's Wisdom value, turn to section 30.

28

The wraith is only a few footsteps away when Alynn finishes the Detect Evil spell. Instantly it is outlined in the telltale green glow. It is evil.

"I could have told you that," Rhea mocks him. "Now watch yourself."

The misty monster surges toward the man. Instinctively the cleric swings his mace. The creature ignores the solid weapon, even though part of its nebulous form is torn away, flowing around it. A numbing cold rolls in waves toward the cleric.

Section 29, 30

Stumbling to one side, Alynn swings the mace again.

Turn to section 35.

29

King Durr waits hunched forward on his throne, his fingers buried in his thinning gray hair. Three days before, Orlow led the massed wizards of the kingdom out to battle the demon Phameet.

The King, a valiant warrior, has always disliked the ways of wizards and priests. He likes waiting on them even less. It had taken all the persuasive skill of his first minister, Talien, to calm him.

The younger man, Talien, dressed in a silk robe, turns to speak to his King but is interrupted by the blast of a trumpet. The warning note is still sounding when the demon's great leg smashes through the wall of the throne room. When it withdraws, dozens of misshapen lesser demons swarm through the opening.

They have their answer. The wizards have failed, and the Darklord is finally triumphant. Exchanging knowing glances, both men draw bejeweled swords and step forward. The King chooses to charge into the ranks of approaching monsters. He disappears into a mass of gaudily colored giant spiders. Talien, always the more careful, retreats to a corner and accounts for two of the demons before he is overwhelmed by sheer numbers.

With Alynn's death, the quest has failed. You can continue the quest until he succeeds. If you desire to improve Alynn's chances for success, allow him an extra Heal Wounds spell.

Turn to section 1.

30

UNDEAD HARPIES
To Hit Alynn: 11   To Be Hit: 12   Hit Points: 7
Damage from Claws: 1 D6

If Alynn wins the combat, turn to section 33. Subtract

Section 31,32

all damage from his total hit points on the record sheet.

If Alynn is killed, turn to section 29.

31

Rising, Alynn puts himself between Lyla and the new menace. The silent creature he just faced makes him more than careful.

"Sure, I'm just going to walk right into your web," he assures the cloudy form. With just a hint of a smile, he begins to chant the Turn Undead spell. As the cleric nears the final phrases, he begins to walk toward the form. It remains where it appeared, unmoving except for the constant flow within its bounds.

While still several steps away, Alynn thrusts forward his talisman and screams out the final words. He can feel the warmth as Cearn's power surges out from his hands. Ahead of him the wraith looks as if it is being buffeted by a fierce wind. It resists for a second as small pieces of cloud are torn away. Painfully it raises its arms as if asking for aid. Before Alynn can react, the wraith tumbles toward the desolate hills and disappears.

No roll for success is needed here, since the wraith did not resist the spell.

Turn to section 40.

32

The wraith hovers near the entrance to the graveyard. For a long moment the living man and his opponent stand facing each other. When Alynn begins the incantation for the Turn Undead spell, the creature reacts.

It oozes. Alynn knows no other word to describe its motion. It moves toward him. Inside its nebulous form, clouds roil. He is reminded of the Mistwall. The wisps are driven to frenzied movement as the wraith gathers its powers to attack. Alynn knows it is necessary for him to believe he can drive away the creature before

Section 33

a Turn Undead spell will work. The cleric wonders how many of his fellows died when doubt overcame their faith.

Involuntarily, Alynn takes a backward step, then another as he finishes the spell. With a shaking hand he prepares to thrust forward his holy symbol.

Roll 3 D6.

If the total is the same as or less than Alynn's value for Wisdom, turn to section 38.

If the total is greater than Alynn's Wisdom value turn to section 35.

33

"They're gone." Rhea's voice breaks the stillness.

"Why didn't you warn me?" the cleric asks angrily.

"I figured that since you found that dark-haired one, you didn't have any need for me." Alynn wonders if he hears a touch of jealousy in the explanation. "I was busy elsewhere," the voice finishes as if in reply to the thought.

"Are you all right?" Lyla asks, grasping his arm. "I was frightened. They were so ugly."

"They're no problem now," Alynn reassures her. It feels good to have shown the dark-haired woman how powerful he is. To have proven to her his abilities.

"You were so taken with her looks you got surprised," Rhea adds deprecatingly.

Lyla stands looking at Alynn. She is smiling slightly, her eyes larger than ever. She seems to be looking up to the cleric, even though she is nearly his height. Trying to find a way to enjoy the woman's obvious adulation without incurring another comment from Rhea, Alynn turns with carefully planned casualness and begins walking toward the hills. Lyla follows and after a few steps links her arm with his. Her presence, the nearness of her hips as they walk, seem to make the throbbing of his wounded shoulder diminish.

The abbey of the Darklord is in a valley. For the last hour, each step they have taken has led them into bleaker surroundings. The plants have become more

Section 33

stunted, their forms grotesque. The shrubs are now a sickly white, twisted as if nearly drained of life. Finally the land nourishes no living thing; no plant, bird, or even insect moves over the dusty hills. The dried vegetation is brown and broken. Even the sunlight is gray and without warmth. It seems as if the sun only reluctantly wastes its light on this accursed land.

After the stark desolation, the abbey looks uncannily familiar. The buildings are virtually identical to those Alynn has left behind. The mortar-and-stone walls and the wooden beams are comforting. While the tan lifeless soil persists, for a few brief moments Alynn is able to throw off the depression the terrain has brought on.

"Well, we made it," he says to Lyla, trying hard to sound optimistic.

"Now for the hard part," Rhea interjects.

"But what waits inside?" Lyla replies.

So much for feeling good, Alynn realizes. This abbey looks the same as his own, but inside waits the Darklord's guardians, and Alynn has to go meet them. The cleric takes the mace from his belt and twists the strap around his wrist.

Still the familiarity lulls his awareness. Near the road is the graveyard. Beyond the Mistwall the graveyard contains the quiet remains of those who have died in Cearn's service. With horror Alynn notices that a misty form rises over the gateway.

The first Alynn knows of the menace is Lyla's scream. Even before it fades Rhea's voice joins the clamor.

"Beware!" In the chaos of the moment Alynn barely notices his ephemeral companion sounds farther away than before. Lyla had been closer to the entrance to the graveyard as they walked past, and the creature had struck at her first. Alynn spins to find her collapsed on the ground, writhing in obvious agony. Poised above the woman is a misty manlike form.

Reflex more than skill brings the mace around, its head swishing through the wraith. As it touches the monster, Alynn hears a shriek, echoing as if in a small room. Both he and the wraith recoil. Between them Lyla lies unmoving on the roadside.

Section 34, 35

If Alynn should cast a Turn Undead spell, turn to section 32.

If Alynn should cast a Heal Wounds spell on Lyla, turn to section 20.

If Alynn should cast a Detect Evil spell, turn to section 24.

If Alynn should engage the apparition in combat, turn to section 35.

34

As always, the Sanctuary spell gives Alynn a sense of well-being. The pleasure of being immune, even for a few minutes to the world's problems has great appeal. It is Lyla's comment that shatters his idyllic mood.

"Hadn't we better hurry?" she asks, eyeing the skeletons patiently waiting just beyond the spell's boundary. "Time is short and sunset close."

Frustrated, the cleric must act. Moving will end the enchantment, but these guards have stood their post for over a century, and waiting a few more minutes will make little difference.

Alynn lifts his mace and steps toward the skeletal guards.

Turn to section 44.

35

WRAITH
To Hit Alynn: 10   To Be Hit: 13   Hit Points: 9
Damage with Touch: Permanently removes 1 hit point from the person touched. He also loses one hit point from his current total. If all points are lost, Alynn is dead.

For example, if Alynn is touched (hit) twice during the melee, he will have a maximum of 13 rather than 15 hit points. This means that even after healing all his wounds Alynn will be able to have only 13 hit points. Change this total on your record sheet.

Section 36

If Alynn defeats the wraith, turn to section 22.

If Alynn is killed, turn to section 29.

36

Lyla hangs back as they enter the stables, or rather what is left of the stables. Alynn can see her eyeing the building as they enter through a collapsed section of one wall. All the walls lean at angles, threatening imminent collapse, and the floor is littered with rotten wood and the remains of long-dead animals.

"Something is missing," Alynn muses. He looks around.

"Rats," Rhea's voice is again distant and garbled as she speaks just the single word.

"Yes, rats," Alynn agrees. "There aren't any rats."

In such a building anywhere else, they would have heard the sound of rats among the debris, one of those sounds you take for granted until it is missing, like the rustle of insects in a forest. Instead, the stables are as silent and lifeless as the area surrounding the abbey. There are not even any cobwebs. Walking into the stables a few steps, the cleric surveys its debris-filled length.

Deciding there is nothing of importance here, Alynn turns to leave. Suddenly, he hears Lyla gasp. Looking at her, he sees that her eyes are large with fear and surprise. Spinning, he faces the threat.

Skeletal hooves are poised ready to strike a few feet over his head. The warhorse whose remains stand before him must once have been enormous, twenty-five hands high, with a chest as wide as a cart. The bones of its legs are as thick as Alynn's arm. Flapping loose on the monster's back is a saddle. Dangling from the saddle horn is a mace. The creature's eyes glow with a hideous red light, bright in the shadowy stable.

Without stopping to consider, Alynn dives away from the slashing hooves, pushing Lyla ahead of him. They fall into a heap among the litter. By the time they untangle themselves, the skeleton is once more poised to strike. No time remains for casting a spell.

Section 37,38

If Alynn should turn and do battle with the skeleton, turn to section 53.

If Alynn should attempt to flee the skeleton, turn to section 59.

37

The corridor is narrow, and by constantly swinging his mace at arm's length, Alynn keeps the skeletons at bay. With their short swords, they are unable to reach past the mace and slash him. Keeping his weapon moving in a rhythmic pattern, he begins to chant the Turn Undead spell.

For a moment, nothing occurs. Then as the chant builds, the skeletons begin to edge back. By its end, the undead guards have backed into the guardrooms. With a firm cry, "By the power of Cearn," Alynn thrusts forward his talisman and strides toward the skeletons.

Roll 3 D6.

If the total is the same as or less than Alynn's Wisdom value, turn to section 54.

If the total is greater than the value of Alynn's Wisdom, turn to section 114. Alynn is distracted by casting the spell and striding toward the skeletons, so they will attack first.

38

"Now you've got it," Rhea's voice intrudes. Her comment has a calm, even casual, sound. It seems to Alynn she already knows he will be successful. Bolstered, he shouts out the final words of the Turn Undead spell and advances on the menace.

The air is still, but the wraith appears to be torn by a fierce gust of wind. The clouds that are its essence stream behind it and disperse. Instead of clutching for Alynn, it now seems to be tearing at itself. Before its scream of agony can be registered, nothing remains.

Cross the Turn Undead spell off your record sheet. Turn to section 22.

Section 39, 40

39

For a moment, nothing occurs. Then as the Turn Undead chant builds strength, the skeletons begin to edge back. By its end, the skeletal guards have been forced off the wall. With a firm invocation, "By the power of Cearn," Alynn holds out his holy symbol and strides toward the skeletons.

Roll 3 D6.

If the total is the same as or less than Alynn's Wisdom value, turn to section 54.

If the total is greater than Alynn's Wisdom value, turn to section 36. Alynn was distracted by casting the spell and striding toward the skeletons, so they will attack first.

40

The walls of the abbey are decayed by time but still standing. The only entrance appears to lead through a twenty-foot tunnel that is blocked by a rusted iron gate. Looking through the dark tunnel, Alynn wonders what terrors might lurk in the passageway. He remembers his shadowy foe, with its chilling touch, at his own abbey. Without realizing it, the cleric pauses several steps from the doorway and stares silently into its blackness.

"Maybe we should try to sneak over the wall?" Lyla suggests.

Her caution reminds Alynn once more that this abbey is a bastion of the evil powers whose liege is the Darklord. Hesitantly, he surveys the walls, half expecting something gruesome to be manning the defenses.

The abbey is surrounded by a wall four times Alynn's height. From the entrance he can see it is at least ten feet thick. Like the rest of the abbey, the walls are covered with crumbling mortar. There are large areas where the thick covering has been battered in some siege. No guards, hideous or human, can be seen on

Section 41

patrol. From here the building appears as desolate as the lands surrounding it. The cleric wonders again at the shriveled plants and lack of even the smallest insects.

"The life force of everything near here has been drained," Rhea informs the cleric matter-of-factly. "Even the most powerful animals were sucked dry by enchantments."

The cleric is worried by her nonchalance. Her voice still seems as if she is speaking to him from a great distance.

"Is something wrong?" he asks. Part of his mind hopes the voice will go away, but another part fears the loss of Rhea's assistance.

"It is harder here," the disembodied voice answers cryptically.

"What is?" Alynn questions, but there is no reply.

If Alynn should go through the entrance, turn to section 49.

If Alynn should climb over the wall, turn to section 52.

41

For a very long second the cleric hangs by one hand. His first thought is that the falling mortar might have injured Lyla. A hurried glance shows her standing, apparently unhurt, among the settling rubble. The tendons of his hand, wedged firmly in a crack in the wall, are already protesting the abuse with every slight sway of his body. The top of the wall is only a scant foot above his handhold.

Weighed down by his mace and chain mail, the Hero fumbles for a foothold. His scrabbling causes him to swing back and forth, like a pendulum, scraping against the wall. The strain on his left wrist produces a burning sensation that promises to blossom quickly into agony.

Hoping his wrist can take a few seconds more of even greater pain, Alynn kicks the air with his legs. The scope of his swing increases, but so does the pain. Lunging upward at the top of a swing, he hooks his

Section 42

free arm over the top of the wall. A leg follows, and the cleric is able to relax his overstrained hand. Panting, he pulls himself onto a narrow walkway that runs along the top of the wall.

Tying his belt to his mace's strap, Alynn hangs over the wall.

"Grab the mace and I'll pull you up," he instructs Lyla.

Without a word, the raven-haired beauty complies. The cleric finds her surprisingly light. Within seconds, the woman stands next to him. Still breathing hard, he bends down to untie the mace. His left wrist throbs painfully.

"Hurry," Lyla says in a panicky voice.

Looking up, Alynn sees the cause of her concern. Moving toward them on the walkway are two skeletons. The unpadded bones rattle awkwardly with each step. One wears a helmet, now too big for its skull and hanging nearly over its eye sockets. The sight would be humorous, Alynn decides, if their swords weren't so steady. Retying his belt, the cleric prepares to meet the unearthly guards.

If Alynn should cast a Turn Undead spell, turn to section 39.

If Alynn should cast a Spirit Hammer spell, turn to section 54.

If Alynn should fight the skeletons, turn to section 114.

42

Alynn hesitates at the entrance to the graveyard. He can't help but wonder if he will ever leave it. The apparition seems friendly, but is not deception the language of all evil? Where is Rhea now that he needs her advice? The memory of the cold and pain comes back. The cleric can hardly bring himself to take the next step.

Then he takes it. To his own surprise, once he begins moving, it becomes easier to approach the creature hovering over the tombstone. Still cautious, he waits for it to speak... or attack.

Section 42

For several seconds the translucent figure seems to be writhing in pain. Parts of the apparition appear to melt and reform. Then the figure seems to gain control of itself, and its form remains constant. It hovers over the grave, nearly transparent in the daylight. Pain is still visible on its features. It waits for the cleric to approach.

"Pain... this is not easy." The apparition speaks as if in great pain.

"What do you want?" Alynn demands with more confidence than he feels.

"Below the abbey," the apparition answers cryptically. "You must not trust her."

The evening breeze begins to rise.

"Who? Why?" the cleric demands, but the form is fading. It grows smaller as if rushing away, but remains perfectly clear. Then, in a very small voice, it speaks again. The first words are lost, and only one phrase is clear.

"...more than she seems..."

Alynn stands staring at the now empty air over the grave. A faint breeze drifts across the graveyard. Dust dances in the no longer stagnant air.

"Don't ask me." Rhea speaks before Alynn can even ask. "Sounds as if he was warning you about your girl friend."

"She is *not* my girl friend!"

"That isn't how you act. Is it necessary to point out even the spirits have warned you about her?"

"Maybe they were warning me about you," he answers, more confused than annoyed. Losing himself in thought, the cleric tries to understand the ghost's warnings. Whoever the ghost had been, it seemed to have appeared at a great cost to itself. One thing was obvious, there was someone or something waiting for him inside the abbey.

By the time Alynn reaches the graveyard gate, Lyla has stood up and is leaning against the wall. Silently she follows him toward the abbey.

Turn to section 40.

43

The tiny hammer seems to grow as it whirls toward the skeletons. As it grows, it becomes less substantial. It is larger than a war hammer and nearly invisible when it reaches the nearest skeletal guard.

The conjured hammer strikes with a thud, followed by the sickening sound of bone splintering. The magic holding the long-dead guard together escapes in a burst of grayish dust. Bones, no longer animated by the Darklord's magic, tumble to the dry ground.

Before the clatter ends, Alynn wields his Spirit Hammer against another skeleton. His efforts are rewarded by the rattle of bones and the ringing of its sword on the ground.

Turning to his third antagonist, the cleric finds a good deal of satisfaction in the ease with which he is sundering the creatures.

"He who hesitates..." Rhea begins to quote an old Gama proverb.

Alynn feels the power of his spell fading. Before he can use it again, the Spirit Hammer dissolves, leaving behind not even his own tiny hammer. Feeling a rush of disappointment after wielding such powerful magic, the cleric prepares to face the remaining skeleton with his mace alone.

Turn to section 44. Alynn has already destroyed two skeletal guards with the spell, so he will have to defeat only one more.

44

SKELETONS
To Hit Alynn: 13   To Be Hit: 10   Hit Points: 3
Damage with Swords: 1 D6

Like most undead, these skeletons will fight until destroyed. All surviving may attack each round.

If Alynn wins the combat, turn to section 46.

If Alynn is killed, turn to section 29.

Section 45

45

The windows in the two low buildings are broken and empty. The cleric tries to not let them remind him of the eye sockets in a skull. He has seen far too many skulls this day, too many of which stared him in the eye while wanting his blood. Still the image won't leave his mind. Cautiously entering the first building, Alynn has trouble overcoming the feeling he is being swallowed by a long-dead giant buried up to its shoulders in rubble.

Inside, the building seems completely harmless and empty. It must have been the dormitory, a large room with cots along the walls. Only the frames remain of the beds, and the tables that ran down the room's center are now barely good for kindling. Lyla points out a few scuff marks in the dust, which warn of a recent visitor, but at first he sees little else. Examining the marks, Alynn decides they must have been made by a barefoot human about the cleric's own size. The woman has already left the building when Alynn notices an object on the floor near the window.

Exactly where a sentinel might be expected to drop a piece of a snack while watching the courtyard through the window, Alynn finds a small cylindrical object. The floor near one end is stained a dark brown. He nearly picks the object up to examine it, when he recognizes it as a human finger. One end has been gnawed, showing the marks of very sharp teeth.

The cleric suddenly feels exposed, and the corners of the room seem dark and full of menace. With a short prayer to Cearn for protection, he hurries out, gesturing for Lyla to follow. If there are cannibals in the abbey, they must be very quiet. Alynn doesn't want them to take him by surprise. He hopes he and Lyla can find the Ankh, if it is here, without alerting the creatures to their presence.

The door to the second building gapes open, barely held upright on rusted hinges. Alert to the danger, Alynn readies his mace before entering. He feels that there is extra menace behind this doorway. Deciding to trust

Section 45

in his instincts, Alynn tears a strip of cloth from his robe and ties it to his mace. Gripping it firmly in both hands, the cleric waves it just inside the door.

The cloth has barely passed the threshold when a clawed hand tears it loose. With a hiss of rage and frustration, a man-sized monster appears in the doorway, the strip of cloth in one filthy hand. Its skin is a dark gray, turning almost as white as putrefying flesh in spots. Its hair is a tangled mass of black bristles. The creature's fingers end in claws, each over an inch long. Its fingers are stained the dark brown of dried blood. Hate and hunger look out at the cleric and the woman through squinting red eyes with black, lusterless pupils. "Not cannibals," the cleric exclaims, "ghouls!"

It takes a special perversity to become a ghoul. The potential ghoul must have an attitude toward death and the dead which is close to worship. Often this is caused by the adult or even a child developing an overwhelming fear of death due to the loss of someone close to them. Death becomes such a force in their life as to become the center of all their thoughts. This worship has to be joined with a deep commitment to evil.

Finally, the mind of the human snaps entirely and the ghoul is born. To become closer to the dead they both fear and envy, they eat dead flesh. The longer dead and more putrefied the flesh, the more satisfying the ghoul finds its meal. Once it begins eating decayed flesh, this craving becomes the dominant part of the ghoul's existence. They begin to frequent graveyards and finally when there are not enough bodies to satisfy them, they create their own.

As the ghoul lives exclusively off dead flesh, it begins to change. Rather than being poisoned by their grisly meals, the ghoul thrives and slowly grows to resemble the very corpses they feast upon. Their skin grows gray and their eyes blank. The only thoughts left are those needed to find ways to satisfy their craving for human flesh. A fully developed ghoul's fingernails will have thickened and hardened to claws. Their canines extend to form short fangs and their bodies exude the sour odor of long dead meat. The final irony is that by a perverse curse the ghoul is given a sort of dark

Section 46

immortality. Once a human is fully changed into a ghoul, it stops aging. Unless slain the ghoul is doomed to never find the death it worshiped and now craves.

The stench of the creature is nearly overpowering. It reeks of rotting flesh and filth. Its slimy gray tongue flicks between jagged yellow teeth. Overwhelmed by disgust, Alynn swings his mace, smashing the creature's skull and shoulder. The blow comes so quickly that the ghoul never even tries to duck. It crumbles with a fading whine of fear and despair. Its mates are eaters of the dead, any dead. Before it has collapsed completely, another ghoul has reached out from beside the doorway and dragged the mortally wounded monster inside to begin ripping at its flesh. Three more of the carrion-eaters emerge from the shadows and cautiously approach the entrance. They spread out into an arc, daring Alynn to enter and face them. They wait, baring their claws and hissing their hunger.

Alynn resolves to stay just outside the doorway, ensuring that only one of the four ghouls can attack him at a time. Lyla, knife drawn, waits behind him. The ghouls, too impatient to wait longer, shuffle toward him.

If Alynn should cast a Turn Undead spell, turn to section 55.

If Alynn should cast a Sanctuary spell, turn to section 58.

If Alynn should fight the ghouls, turn to section 62.

46

Someone or something is watching them. Alynn doesn't know quite how he is sure of that, but somehow he knows. Added to the gruesome encounters he has already had in this abandoned abbey, the feeling makes him very nervous. Carefully placing his back to the wall near the entrance, he braces himself for another battle. Lyla, a few feet to his left, does the same. The slight wind stirs the gray dust, but nothing else moves.

Section 46

After several silent minutes pass, she gives him an inquiring look. Alynn realizes the nervous feeling has passed. He makes a final scan of the deserted courtyard, shrugs, and tries to smile. The sun is low, and both know the time is growing short. Tonight the Darklord will open the gate.

Dominating the abbey is the temple, a large stone building with few windows. Like all temples of Cearn it resembles a fort more than a place of worship. In the past, Alynn had found the security of the solidly built temples appealing. Only here, the thick walls and narrow, high windows remind him of how defenseless he and Lyla are against the legendary might of the Darklord. To their left are the abandoned stables. The doors are missing, and the thatch of its roof has blown away. To the right stand two buildings. In the Lesser Abbey, they housed the brothers and any travelers. These structures, Alynn reminds himself, may harbor anything. The hint of movement in a window of the nearest building catches Alynn's eye. Gripping his mace firmly, the cleric stands unmoving and watches the windows. Noticing his scrutiny, Lyla draws her dagger and stands poised beside him.

After a long minute he relaxes slightly, wondering if he really saw something or if he just imagined it, as he had imagined hearing voices. Nothing appears to have moved, but the pause has given his wrist, shoulder, and back the opportunity to remind him of the painful hazards he has already faced. He grimaces and relaxes his grip on the mace.

"We're both exhausted—and nervous," Lyla comments understandingly.

"And after all, you are hearing voices," Rhea taunts him over the silence of the empty courtyard. "Well, mine anyhow," she finishes in a friendly tone. The cleric notices Rhea's voice sounds happier and firmer than earlier. Alynn finds himself chuckling. If he is just hearing voices, at least he hasn't lost his sense of humor.

Lyla turns and looks at him. Fighting the urge to shrug self-consciously again, Alynn settles for trying to look courageous. He walks forward in a purposeful manner.

Now that he has taken the initiative, it becomes necessary to choose where they will go. A silent appeal to Rhea for guidance brings no reply.

If Alynn should go to the stables, turn to section 36.

If Alynn should go to the residences, turn to section 45.

If Alynn should go to the temple, turn to section 57.

47

The corridor is narrow, so by swinging his mace at arm's length, Alynn keeps the skeletons at bay. Their short swords seem unable to reach him. Keeping the mace moving in a rhythmic pattern, he begins to chant the Spirit Hammer spell.

Chanting the harsh-sounding words of the spell, the cleric gropes in a pocket for the tiny hammer needed to make the spell function. Splitting his attention, he is barely able to dodge a sword thrust under his flailing mace. Then he grasps the hammer and finishes the spell.

With a smooth motion Alynn tosses the hammer at the nearest guard.

Roll 3 D6.

If the total is the same as or less than the cleric's Wisdom value, turn to section 43.

If the total is greater than the value of Alynn's Wisdom, the spell has failed. Turn to section 44.

48

The hooves plunge heavily downward. The cleric attempts to crack the horse's vulnerable bones with his mace. The end of one leg splinters as the weapon glances across it. The momentum of the mace carries it up over Alynn's left shoulder. Before he can reverse the weapon, one massive hoof smashes into the cleric's chest. The impact sends him spinning. He sprawls face

Section 49

down on the rough floor.

Before the Hero can turn over, the hooves smash down again, bringing the full weight of hundreds of pounds of bone crashing into his spine. Alynn hears the crack at the same time as he feels the wrenching jar.

It is less pain than a terrible change which registers in the man's mind. His spine has shattered at the waist, and he is unable even to turn and face the long-dead monster. Sooner than he might expect, a hoof smashes into his shoulder, and the useless mace drops from numb fingers.

The final blow crashes into the back of the cleric's head with a burst of color and a surge of agony.

Turn to section 29.

49

As they approach the entrance, Alynn notices there is no wound on Lyla. Even her robe is untorn. The attack that knocked her down doesn't even seem to have produced a bruise. He is still looking at her when she stops and points. Following her gesture, the cleric sees vague lettering, obscured by time, over the entrance:

THE ABBEY OF CEARN
THE PROTECTOR

Alynn reads the name with more than a little astonishment. He had spent years in the Lesser Abbey and never wondered if there was a Greater Abbey. To him it had always just been a name.

"For over five hundred years Cearn was worshiped here," Rhea says in a strangely distant and controlled voice. "The abbey was a center for learning and sheltered the greatest men of the day. It took the minions of the Darklord three months to defeat the defenders, even after he cut them off from any hope of outside help. When the wall was finally breached, the defenders resisted until the last.

"Just before that siege a small group of brothers was sent to summon aid. They failed to return in time and

Section 49

so instead founded the Lesser Abbey. One of them was the Wizard who created the Ankh you seek."

"How could you know all this?" Alynn asks the voice. There is no reply, but he feels a nearly overwhelming sense of loss and frustration pass over him. In less time than it takes to be aware of the feelings they pass.

Shaking himself free of the powerful emotions, Alynn strides into the ten-foot-long corridor that serves as the only entrance to the fortified abbey. The far gate appears to have been burned through, and nothing blocks his way but a few scraps of charred timber.

In the dim light of the tunnel, they nearly fail to notice the darker blots that are the entrances to the guardrooms. Not until he sees the glint of a sword emerging from a doorway does the cleric become aware of the danger. Stopping abruptly, he has the satisfaction of watching the sword jab ineffectually a few inches in front of him. Backing up another step, he raises his mace and prepares to meet the ambushers.

After encountering so many other undead, the emergence of the skeletons is hardly a surprise. Lyla moves carefully behind him, nearly backing out of the entranceway.

"Be careful," she warns. Alynn is pleased with her concern, though he has little time to dwell on it. Three skeletons now block his path. Each is clad in rusty armor and a tattered robe. On one robe the Hero can make out the faded symbol of Cearn. These were once the defenders of the abbey. Now they are still at their post, but serving the Darklord. Perhaps they still remember something of their former loyalties.

"I am a priest of Cearn," he announces with as steady a voice as possible. "Let me pass."

The skeletal guards stand unmoving. Alynn keeps the mace ready. Then, to his amazement, the skeletons begin to edge back against the wall.

Relieved, the cleric turns to gesture for Lyla to follow him. Out of the corner of an eye he sees a sword slash toward him. Awkwardly he brings up the mace, catching the blade on its handle. Within seconds the other skeletons join the attack.

"Nice try," Rhea comments, sounding amused. Alynn

is too busy to care.

If Alynn should cast a Turn Undead spell, turn to section 37.

If Alynn should cast a Spirit Hammer spell, turn to section 47.

If Alynn should use his Sanctuary spell, turn to section 34.

If Alynn should fight the skeletons, turn to section 44.

50

For a very long second the cleric hangs by one hand. His first thought is that the falling mortar might have injured Lyla. A hurried glance shows her standing among the rubble below, apparently unhurt. Then even his precarious handhold gives way. With a moan of frustration, he slides down the rough wall, the jagged edges of the exposed rock tearing at his legs and chain mail. The jolt of landing mingles with the sharp jabs from the broken stone and mortar. The muscles of one leg and in his back immediately protest. Within seconds he feels as if invisible demons are digging tiny daggers into his lower back. Considering where he is, the idea does not seem impossible. Alynn catches himself glancing behind him, then laughs at his own fears.

Alynn has received 2 hit points of damage from the fall. Subtract these from his total hit points on your record sheet.

If Alynn should try to climb the wall again, turn to section 52.

If Alynn should go through the entrance to the abbey, turn to section 49.

51

It appears to Lyla as if some unseen hand sweeps up the long dead guards and smashes them to the dry ground below. The sound of splintering bone is loud, and swords rattle against the wall. Dust rises, obscur-

Section 52

ing her view. When the dust clears, nothing remains beyond shards of bone, two bent swords, and the remnants of armor.

Alynn and Lyla glance hurriedly around, but the noise seems to have attracted no attention. Alynn tries not to think of the returning silence as deathlike.

Could these have been the only guards at this abbey? Alynn wonders hopefully.

"Hardly," comes the dry reply from within his mind somewhere. "Be on guard, but hurry!"

Grasping his mace and favoring his throbbing left wrist, the cleric leads the way down the stairs at one end of the wall. He and Lyla emerge in a courtyard near the inside end of the dark passageway they had avoided. The thought of fighting a skeleton or worse in those close quarters sends a shudder up Alynn's spine. Seeing a look of worry on Lyla's face, he tries to give the woman his most confident smile.

Turn to section 46.

52

Time and the wind have eroded the wall and produced hundreds of cracks and holes in its surface. Alynn finds he can wedge his toes and fingers into these fairly easily. Strapping his mace to his waist, he begins to climb. Very quickly the cleric discovers the mortar crumbles under his weight. Climbing the wall becomes a race in which he tries to move on to the next foothold before the one he is using gives way.

The day is not warm, but the cleric can feel wetness spreading across his shoulders and back. Looking down, he sees Lyla below, her face reflecting concern. The mace bangs painfully against his legs with every movement, but there is little he can do about it. He has nearly reached the top when the ancient wall under both feet gives way. A three-foot section of mortar tears free and crashes to the ground below.

Roll 3 D6.

If the total is the same as or less than Alynn's Dexterity

Section 53, 54

value, turn to section 41.

If the total is greater than Alynn's Dexterity value, turn to section 50.

53

SKELETON WARHORSE
To Hit Alynn: 12   To Be Hit: 11   Hit Points: 8
Damage per round: 1 D6 total from Hooves and Bite

If Alynn defeats the skeleton, turn to section 60.

If Alynn is killed, turn to section 48.

54

It appears to Lyla that some unseen hand sweeps up the long-dead guards and smashes them against the walls of the entranceway. The sound of splintering bone is loud in the closed space. Dust and rocks fall from the ceiling, obscuring her view. When the dust clears, nothing remains beyond shards of bone, bent swords, and remnants of armor.

Pleased with the success of his spell, Alynn walks purposefully out into the courtyard. Glancing around, he sees no other obvious threats and gestures for Lyla to follow. A short time later the couple stand blinking in the sunlit courtyard.

The temple towers over the two humans. As he scans the building and courtyard, Alynn can feel his confidence wane. Cautiously he edges away from the dark entranceway until his back is protected by the wall. All Alynn can think of is how many skeletons, zombies and other creatures it can hold. Lyla, too, seems awed by the size of the temple and abbey. For several minutes both stand watching the shadows caused by the setting sun grow longer. Neither seems to relish the concept of being trapped in the abandoned abbey after dark. Alynn also realizes they have no choice. Unless they intervene tonight, the gate will be opened and this world will succumb to the Darklord.

Turn to section 46.

Section 55

55

It is hard to concentrate on the Turn Undead spell while a noisome ghoul is trying to get past your mace and rake you with its claws. Alynn cannot get into the rhythm of the chant necessary to bring forth the might of Cearn and drive the undead monsters away.

Just as he must begin again for the third time, a new attack by the beast forces him to concentrate on defending himself. Snarling and hissing, four of the monsters crowd forward, anxious to share in the human feast.

Fearing one of those claws will reach him while he is busy casting the spell, Alynn reasons he must stand and meet the creatures in hand-to-hand combat. Outnumbered four to one, he has only a slim chance of success. The dagger flying past his shoulder changes the situation drastically.

Lyla's dagger buries itself in the eye socket of the ghoul he has been fighting. Alynn brings the mace around in a forceful swing from the waist. It brushes easily past a mottled arm thrown out to block it, crunching into the monster's head. The ghoul falls, twitching and bleeding gray ooze at Alynn's feet. The grave robber behind it ignores the cleric while it drags the ghoul's body away, tearing into it with pointed teeth. For a few seconds the ghouls jostle each other for a piece of their unfortunate comrade.

During the respite, Alynn tries once more to gain the mental balance needed to concentrate on the spell. This time he begins to feel the familiar surge of power. With growing confidence he hurries through the chant, ending with a loud "By the power of Cearn."

The ghouls' hisses turn to squeals of terror as an unseen force propels them away from the cleric. Within seconds the creatures have been driven across the wide hall and jammed against the far wall. Screaming their hate and frustration, the ghouls squeeze along the wall and escape out a window. From outside Lyla sees the monsters tumble out of the abbey still screeching in panic.

Turn to section 61.

Section 56

56

The first ghoul rushes through the doorway, arms extended. Often enough, the pure horror of such an attack must have served to freeze a victim motionless, but Alynn has seen too much in a short time to be so easily cowed. He brings the mace around in a solid swing from the waist. It brushes easily past a mottled arm thrown out to block it, and crunches into the monster's chin. The ghoul falls, twitching and bleeding gray ooze at Alynn's feet, its chin and mouth now a smashed ruin. The ghoul tries to shriek its pain and anger, but only a rattling gurgle emerges from what remains of its mouth.

The second ghoul rushes at him directly behind the first. It nearly reaches Alynn as he struggles to bring the heavy mace around. Just then a familiar knife appears in its stomach. It doubles over in agony and surprise. The cleric grunts his thanks to Lyla as he brings the mace down on the confused ghoul's neck. With its head nearly torn loose, it falls over the writhing body of its comrade.

Just before the third ghoul reaches him, Alynn takes one step back. The monster continues its mindless advance and finds its legs tangled in the bodies of its fellows. Taking advantage of the creature's predicament, the hero smashes his mace into one of its legs. The ghoul stumbles backward, hissing from the pain. The cleric follows it and raises his mace. A blood-covered hand darts upward and tears across his face. A sear of white-hot pain is followed by the dark stickiness of blood pouring from the wound.

Blinded, Alynn can hear the wounded ghoul scramble to its feet. Blood still streams into the Hero's eyes. He can hardly see the claws as they reach toward his throat. He never notices the dagger thunking into the beast's shoulder. With an angry grunt of pain, the ghoul retreats.

As Alynn struggles to wipe the blood from his eyes, he glimpses another ghoul diving at him from the shadows. Lyla's scream of warning coincides with the grave robber's impact. Both tumble to the floor.

Locked together with the monster, Alynn cannot use his mace. He is effectively disarmed, but the ghoul has its teeth and claws. As he struggles to push the carrion-eater off, blood blinds him. The slash that tears into his throat elicits a scream of pain which ends in a breathless gurgle. Alynn feels the yellowed claws punch through the soft skin of his neck and the warmth of fresh blood pouring from it. His last sight is the ghoul's face wrinkled in a parody of a smile as it bends to rend his throat. He tries to warn Lyla to flee, but the blackness rushes in.

Turn to section 29.

57

A survey shows Alynn that the main temple is laid out in the traditional style. Since all temples of Cearn often have to serve as a refuge, they are constructed so as to be easily defended. This building has only one entrance and the few windows are narrow and set high above their heads.

The doors stand twice Alynn's height and over fifteen feet across. A keyhole choked with rust is visible in the center. Resigning himself to entering through the doors and facing any ambush readied at so likely a route, Alynn leans against one of the massive oaken panels and pushes. Heave as he might, the cleric cannot get either door to open.

"Perhaps I can help," Lyla suggests, "We Gama have developed some skill at opening locked doors."

The cleric nods his assent and stands back. Lyla approaches the lock and then examines it carefully.

"Hadn't you better watch our backs while I do this?" she asks pointedly.

"Sure," Alynn agrees, turning and facing the courtyard with his mace held ready. Except for a low murmur from Lyla, the cold silence continues. Even the breeze has died, leaving the abbey as still as the macabre painting of a mad artist in the red light of the setting sun.

"It's open now," Lyla announces, sounding proud of

Section 57

herself. Taking a step back, the hero presses his shoulders against the door. He nearly stumbles when it opens easily. Before he can regain his balance, it smashes with a resounding crash against the wall.

Nervously Alynn surveys the room to see whose attention the noise may have attracted. He holds his mace ready and tries to remember which spells he has used this day. To his relief the large room is as devoid of movement as the courtyard. Lyla must have a most subtle touch, he tells himself, noticing the rust blocking the old keyhole has been barely disturbed.

"Well, they know you're here," Rhea comments acidly. "Have you thought of ringing the temple bells as well?"

"We had better hurry," Lyla insists, simultaneously.

Without replying to either, Alynn walks toward the altar in the center of the temple hall. The room itself is larger than any building along the border. Only in Terverni, the capital city, has the cleric seen any like it. The roof is lined with copper plates, making the dimming sunlight angling through the high windows even redder.

Two small doors are visible. One is in the far right corner, beyond the altar. The second is in the left wall even with the altar. Both are closed.

The altar itself dominates the area. It is covered in intricately worked bronze. On each side of the altar Alynn knows there will be an image of Cearn in his armor protecting his followers from danger. By tradition, the front of the altar will show Cearn warding off death; on the back he will fight against evil; on the left, natural disasters; and on the right, disease.

In the dim light it isn't until he approaches to within a few dozen feet of the altar that the cleric notices the stone casket partially recessed in the floor. Its cover bears the sign of Cearn, a double ankh on a round shield.

"The Ankh you seek is far below the temple." Rhea's voice is barely audible. It sounds to Alynn as if her voice is muffled by the roar of a strong wind. "A scroll of great power lies in the grave before you."

"We should not disturb the dead," Lyla comments,

Section 57

joining Alynn near the casket.

"He is the founder of the order—my order—if there are any more of us left."

"It that's what's in the grave. It's been a long time," Lyla warns. "Anything could be there now."

"I have reason to believe there is a scroll in there."

"How do you know?"

"I just know," he answers vaguely. Lyla is obviously upset at the evasion.

"You could wait at the entrance while I open the casket," Alynn offers.

His suggestion just seems to upset the woman even more. Shrugging her shoulders, she bends over and grasps the handle. When the cover proves too heavy for her to lift, Alynn joins her in the effort. The cover gives with a sudden snap and then pulls up easily.

Inside the stone casket is a body wrapped around and around with narrow strips of cloth. The arms are folded across its chest, protecting a silver cylinder. Engraved on the cylinder is the double Ankh of Cearn. Alynn pauses before reaching in to take the scroll case, hoping this body will not suddenly animate. Gesturing Lyla to step back, he watches the cloth-covered figure for any sign it might be a threat.

Nothing.

He waits another dozen heartbeats.

Still nothing. No movement or anything to indicate that the mummy is a threat.

"Rhea, are you sure?" Alynn asks, without speaking aloud.

Silence.

"Rhea?" This time he speaks out loud.

"Who?" Lyla asks softly.

Still no answer, only stillness inside the casket. Alynn knows that to take the case is likely to cause trouble, but the tension of waiting, trying to decide whether to take it or not, becomes unbearable. Better to have it done and continue, he decides.

Finally Alynn reaches for the scroll. His hand shakes as it moves slowly toward the case. His senses rise to near painful acuteness. The cleric feels the slight movement of air against his skin. He hears Lyla's soft

Section 57

breathing and the rapid beat of his own heart. A spot in the center of his back chooses now to begin itching with vengeful fury.

He grasps the silver case.

When his fingers touch it, the mummy's shrouded hands twitch toward his arm.

Roll 3 D6.

If the total is the same as or less than Alynn's Dexterity value, turn to section 63.

If the total is greater than Alynn's value for Dexterity, turn to section 66.

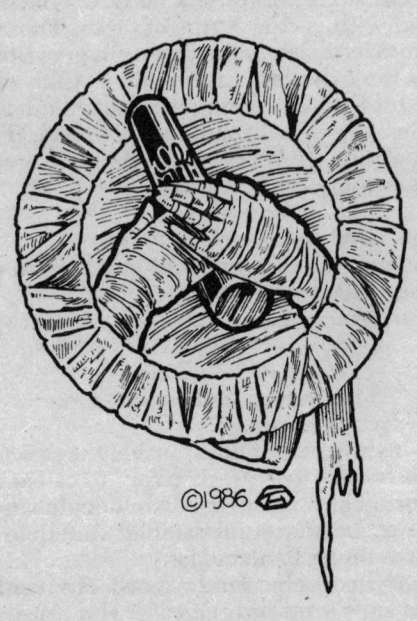

Section 58

58

The first ghoul rushes through the doorway, arms extended. Often enough, the pure horror of such an attack must have served to freeze a victim motionless, but Alynn has seen too much in a short time to be so easily cowed. He brings the mace around in a forceful swing from the waist. It brushes easily past a mottled arm thrown out to block it and crunches into the monster's chin. The ghoul falls, twitching and bleeding gray ooze at Alynn's feet, its chin and mouth now a smashed ruin. The ghoul tries to shriek its pain and anger, but only a rattling gurgle emerges from what remains of its mouth.

The invocation of the Sanctuary spell requires only a brief chant, uttered in haste more often than not. Alynn is able to blurt out the spell before the next grave robber can get close enough to attack. Almost instantly the cleric recognizes the feeling of warmth and security the spell brings to its caster. He finds himself smiling at the ghoul, which is poised to strike only a few feet in front of him. The excitement of the recent combat and the feeling of euphoria and well-being that accompanies a Sanctuary spell serve to change Alynn's smile into a gigantic grin.

The grin infuriates the gruesome beast, and it jumps toward the cleric, claws extended. Its howl of attack turns to a startled yelp as it crashes against the invisible barrier. A second dive, harder than the first, leaves it sitting stunned a few feet inside the door. Knowing he and Lyla are at least temporarily safe, Alynn can't resist a barking laugh at the ghoul's situation.

Now raging, the ghoul screams with frustration. Those behind it edge forward and themselves strike the magical barrier. The first ghoul begins to drag away the body of their fallen comrade. By the time the others realize they cannot reach the grinning cleric, the first ghoul is in a corner tearing mouthfuls of flesh from the body's arm. With growls of anger, the others abandon Alynn and hurry over to share in the feast.

"A good time to leave," Lyla suggests. "After eating,

Section 59

they will be torpid for several days." Without a word Alynn backs cautiously out the door. The ghouls are now totally engrossed in dismembering their former companion and do not try to follow.

Turn to section 61.

59

The monster drives the cleric farther back with each flailing strike of its massive hooves. Dust and small boards fall from the walls each time the beast smashes at the ground. Alynn cannot strike at the monster's head without placing himself in range of its slashing hooves.

Still backing away, Alynn nearly stumbles over a pile of fallen shingles. After a few unbalanced steps backward, he finds a fallen roof beam blocking his retreat. The skeletal warhorse continues advancing upon him. Recovering his balance against the beam, the cleric dives to one side to avoid a killing blow.

"Straight back! Run!" Lyla shouts from behind him. Ducking another descent of the skeletal legs, Alynn backs quickly away.

The warhorse follows, but stops abruptly at the doorway of the decrepit stable. There it shakes its head as if to whinny a challenge, and the glow in its eyes flashes ominously, but it does not advance into the courtyard. Cautiously Alynn backs away from the creature. To his surprise Lyla, so frightened when the battle began, seems quite calm now.

"It cannot leave the stable," she explains. "It was set by the master of this place to guard that area. If it leaves, it will lose the false life the master has given it."

"How do you know that?" Alynn asks the woman. She had shown her skill with a knife in the battle with the Orcs. Now she was speaking with casual knowledge of the undead. Why had she agreed to join so hopeless a quest?

"About time you started thinking," Rhea commends.

"We Gama have learned much about the ways of darkness," Lyla explains smoothly. "We are travelers, and many stories are told at our gatherings. What one

Section 60

has learned we all know soon."

"Makes sense," Alynn corrects Rhea in his mind. "You're still jealous."

"Fool," the spirit voice answers.

"You are jealous," the cleric argues. "You're jealous of my interest in a human woman. One I can touch and feel." The excitement of combat has not yet cooled, and Alynn says this with more vehemence than he intends.

The silence that follows worries him. The cleric is tempted to apologize or at least call to Rhea to see if she is still there. Pride prevents him from doing so. He resents missing Rhea, he discovers, almost as much as he fears to continue without her help. Then he looks at the imposing bulk of the temple.

"Look, I'm sorry," he finally thinks at her, but there is no reply. Lyla walks over and holds on to his arm, but even with her near, the cleric feels very alone.

Turn to section 61.

60

The monster drives the cleric farther back with each flailing strike of its massive hooves. Dust and small boards fall from the walls each time the beast smashes at the ground. Alynn cannot strike at the monster's head without placing himself within range of its slashing hooves.

Still backing away, Alynn nearly stumbles over a pile of fallen shingles. After a few unbalanced steps backward, he finds a fallen roof beam blocking his retreat. The skeletal warhorse continues advancing upon him. Recovering his balance against the beam, the cleric dives to one side to avoid a killing blow.

Seeking an opportunity, Alynn continues to move forward until he is beside the raging skeletal horse. Its bones are cracked and dry. They grate loudly with each movement, and the horse can hardly turn its head. All the monster's attacks are toward its front. Standing by its side Alynn has a few instants' grace. He uses them to raise the mace high over his head, bringing it down onto the skeleton's vulnerable spine.

Section 61

Bone splinters and cracks. Though it cannot utter a sound, the cleric feels rather than hears its scream of anguish. The head creaks around, and yellowed, broken teeth snap closed inches from his face. Even while avoiding them, he swings his mace down again on the same section of ancient bone.

This time the spine parts at a vertebra. Its integrity lost, the creature's attack ends in a clatter of falling bone. For seconds bits of plaster and rotten wood shower from the walls, and then silence rules again.

Alynn reaches across the no longer threatening bones and lifts the mace from the brittle leather of the saddle. On its handle are the symbols that a cleric of Cearn would inscribe on an enchanted mace. The handle seems solid, and the head is firmly attached. Weighing the weapon in one hand, he considers whether or not to keep it.

Lyla, who had fled outside through the hole in the wall, cautiously peeks around. Alynn gives her a proud if somewhat shaky smile. He hopes she will find it reassuring.

"It could be cursed. That was no cleric's mount," Lyla warns, eyeing the weapon.

If Alynn wishes to keep the mace, turn to section 105.

If he wishes to leave the mace behind, turn to section 61.

61

"We are no closer to the Ankh," Lyla observes in a level tone.

"I have no idea where it might be," Alynn admits. "This place is in some ways similar to my abbey... what was mine, but in other ways this one is different." He looks around the deserted courtyard and at the towering temple. Even before it fell, an abbey so big would have its own secret places. "There must be many things here of which I know nothing."

"It is close, very close," Rhea interjects, her voice again sounding distant and strained.

"You're fading," Alynn warns, somewhat relieved to

hear from her.

"I'm afraid it will get worse," Rhea warns.

Hoping to hear some hint of what to do next, Alynn waits. Seconds pass, then a minute. He concentrates harder, hoping to hear some sound inside his head. He hears only the throbbing of his heart and his ragged breathing.

"Standing here and staring will get us nowhere," Lyla interrupts impatiently.

If Alynn should investigate the stables, turn to section 36.

If Alynn should investigate the residences, turn to section 45.

If Alynn should investigate the temple, turn to section 57.

62

GHOULS
To Hit Alynn: 13   To Be Hit: 10   Hit Points: 5
Damage each round: 1 D6 with Claws or Teeth, plus Paralyze

Each time a ghoul succeeds in hitting the Hero, there is a chance that Alynn will be paralyzed for the next round. To determine this, roll 3 D6 each time Alynn is hit. If the total is greater than Alynn's value for Constitution, he is paralyzed. This means he may not attack on the next round, and the ghoul has a +2 to hit him.

Since Alynn is standing just outside the doorway, only one ghoul at a time may attack. When one falls, the next will take its place until all four are slain.

If Alynn defeats the ghouls, turn to section 67.

If Alynn is killed, turn to section 56.

63

The mummy's arms actually creak as they move. Even more quickly Alynn pulls back his hand. Dust

Section 64

rises from the ancient rags as the shrouded hands grab at him. The silver scroll case rattles to the floor as the mummy's ancient form rises slowly and starts toward the humans.

"Stay back," Lyla warns, backing toward the entrance. "Its touch can cause disease."

Quickly taking her advice, Alynn hefts his mace. The mummy is covered in strips of graying cloth. Its face is covered by a thin veil behind which a soft green light is glowing with a sickly luminescence. Alynn decides he would just as soon not discover what the veil hides. The air fills with the sickly sweet odor of embalming fluids. The monster's feet scuff along the dusty floor as it moves to pursue the retreating couple.

Turn to section 66.

64

They both hesitate at the door. At eye level are a pair of handprints looking as if someone dipped his hands in fresh blood and then leaned against the door. The dark red liquid glistens as if fresh. It smears when Alynn scrapes at it with his mace. Exchanging glances, the cleric and his companion free their weapons. Then Alynn pushes tentatively against the thick door while careful not to touch the handprints or the bloody rivulets running from them.

There are no windows in the room beyond this door. In the light of the doorway three more doors are visible in the left wall. On the far wall is the barely visible outline of another door. Patches of blood stain the floor. Out of morbid curiosity the cleric glances at the inside of the door he has just opened, but neither handprints nor any other marks are visible.

Stepping into the room, Alynn releases the door. It begins to swing shut. As the room darkens, he feels a rush of panic and backs up quickly to hold it open. Lyla, who has not yet entered the room, retreats quickly until she is clear of the doorway.

"What is it?" she asks from outside the room.

Alynn gestures for silence, stepping outside. He uses his mace to hold the door open.

Section 65

Both hear a sound like the intake of a breath, but nothing moves in the darkness. Inching the door open wider, the humans peer anxiously into the half-light. The other doors remain closed, and nothing moves.

For long seconds they wait. Finally Lyla tears a strip of cloth from the bottom of her robe and uses it to wedge the door open a few inches. Assured of at least some light, they take a few steps into the room. With a disconcerting thunk, the door slams closed behind them.

Nearly diving, Alynn drags open the door. The strip of cloth is unwound across the floor several feet from the doorway. No one and nothing can be seen in the temple area. Cautiously, the cleric searches around the only corner where an opponent might be hiding, but finds nothing.

When he returns, Lyla has backed out of the room, and the door has once more swung closed. She is breathing deeply and staring at the handprints.

"Something moved," she warns in clipped tones. "Something in the corner. Then the door closed again."

"We have to hurry." Alynn remembers Rhea's warning. The temple is lit now by the gray of twilight. The corners of the large hall are growing as ominously dark as the room before them. For a moment, they say nothing. Then Lyla reaches once more for the door.

If Alynn should cast a Light spell before crossing the room, turn to section 65.

If they should cross the room in darkness, turn to section 73.

65

Gesturing for Lyla to wait, the cleric of Cearn begins to chant. After a few seconds the head of his mace begins to glow. As the chant grows in intensity and volume, the mace glows more brightly. Only when the light is as bright as daylight does Alynn end the Light spell.

The security of the bright glow restores much of Alynn's confidence. He remembers the creatures they

Section 65

have faced aready and how each has been defeated. His fellow clerics would be amazed at the heroic efforts of their least adventurous brother. The thought of his lost friends saddens him, but he finds renewed confidence in the weight of the mace. He still can prevent the Darklord from benefiting from their slaughter. In the center of a pool of brightness, they reenter the room.

Illuminated by the magical light, the hall seems smaller and less threatening. There are two doors at the far side and three doors on their left. From the vents at the bottom, Alynn knows those on the left lead to storage closets. He once helped build similar closets at the Lesser Abbey. The plans they had used were old, perhaps based on the memory of these closets. He knows it is unlikely there will be any escape route through them.

Lyla's intake of breath causes him to spin around. Her eyes wide, the woman points at the inside of the door through which they had entered the room. A second set of handprints has appeared. They look to have been burned into the wood. Alynn is still studying the prints when the first of the shadows begins to glide along the ceiling toward him. Seeing the movement, Alynn spins, half crouched with his mace ready.

The dark dwellers are easily visible in the magical light. They are roughly man-shaped, but with no true substance of their own. As they move into the circle of brightness, each hesitates and seems to struggle with the light. It is only after the second monster enters the brightness that the first continues. Then both act with surprising and nearly deadly swiftness.

Their measured flow becomes a dash. Alynn is barely able to bring around his mace before they are hovering near his head. There is no time to chant a spell. It is all the cleric can do to avoid the darting thrusts of darkness and drive them back with his glowing mace. The shadows' aggressiveness forces the Hero to back away. The dark forms follow.

SHADOWS
To Be Hit (in light): 10   To Hit Alynn: 11   Hit Points: 7

Damage: 1 point of Strength lost each time Alynn is hit

If Alynn's Strength value is lowered to 5 or less, he can do only 1 hit point of damage per hit with the mace. If his Strength value is lowered to zero, he is killed. A shadow cannot be harmed by a nonmagical weapon. If Alynn does not have a magical weapon, turn to section 107. There are two shadows.

If Alynn defeats the shadows, turn to section 78.

If Alynn is killed, turn to section 72.

If he wins, at the end of the combat Alynn's strength is restored to normal.

66

Heat, not pain, is the first sensation the cleric feels. Where those cloth-covered hands wrap around his wrist and arm, the skin feels as if it is being seared away. His howl of agony echoes and fills the temple.

Alynn lunges back from the casket. His fingers are still curled around the scroll, more automatically than deliberately.

Alynn receives one hit point of damage from the mummy's touch. Subtract this on the record sheet. Since he has also been wounded by a mummy, Alynn will be subject to the possible effects of disease.

Turn to section 71.

67

The first ghoul rushes through the doorway, arms extended. Often enough, the pure horror of such an attack must have served to freeze a victim motionless, but Alynn has seen too much in a short time to be so easily cowed. He brings the mace around in a forceful swing from the waist. It brushes easily past a mottled arm thrown out to block it, and crunches into the monster's chin. The ghoul falls, twitching and bleeding gray ooze at Alynn's feet, its chin and mouth now a smashed ruin. The ghoul tries to shriek its pain and anger, but only a rattling gurgle emerges from what remains of its mouth.

Section 67

The second ghoul rushes at him directly behind the first. It nearly reaches Alynn as he struggles to bring the heavy mace around. Just then a familiar knife appears in its stomach. It doubles over in agony and surprise. The cleric grunts his thanks to Lyla as he brings the mace down on the confused ghoul's neck. With its head nearly torn loose, it falls over the writhing body of its comrade.

Just before the third ghoul reaches him, Alynn takes one step back. The monster continues its mindless advance and finds its legs tangled in the bodies of its fellows. Taking advantage of the creature's predicament, the hero smashes his mace into one of its legs. The ghoul stumbles backward, hissing from the pain. The cleric follows it and lands a solid blow on its right shoulder. A final blow to the skull causes it to crumple, sprawling a few feet inside the room.

This building consists of one large room lined with cots. The last ghoul waits on the far side of the dormitory. Its face and chest are smeared with the blood of its fallen companion. As Alynn enters the dimly lit hall, it hisses possessively. Tearing an arm from the body, the ghoul retreats into a corner.

This one, Alynn notices, is smaller than the others. It had never struck him that a child could become a ghoul. For a second he hesitates to strike, reluctant to kill a child, even one as hideous and repulsive as this. As he pauses, the monster swings at him with the arm it wrenched from the body of its comrade. The blood smears across the cleric's chain mail. Unthinking, Alynn swings a counterblow that lands with a smack against the neck of the young ghoul. Its spine breaks with an audible snap.

Alynn looks at the fallen creature with disgust. For a man who has dedicated ten years to saving the lives of others, he is becoming depressingly skilled at killing. The wages of battle seem less glorious, and he feels soiled. Turning away, he sees Lyla pulling her dagger free from the body near the entrance. He feels thanks are appropriate, but can't bring himself to talk. She sees his expression, surveys the room with a quick glance. Offering a sympathetic nod, she moves quickly

Section 68

out of sight. Looking once more at the ghoul-child, the cleric feels nauseated. He hurries to a window and breathes deeply, glad Lyla can't see his weakness. Several numb minutes later, Alynn joins her in the courtyard.

Turn to section 61.

68

The mummy advances slowly. The arms extend forward. After a few steps Alynn sees the creature is moving toward Lyla, not him. The woman has drawn her knife. The dark-haired woman darts the cleric a questioning glance.

In backing away, they have been separated by several steps. The mummy is moving with surprising speed despite its shuffling walk. The green emanating from its face is growing brighter. If Alynn is to stop it from reaching Lyla, he knows he must act now.

The chant for the Turn Undead spell doesn't feel right as Alynn recites the words. He knows he is making the right sounds, but the feeling of growing power is missing. Hesitantly, the cleric begins again. Lyla continues to back away from the mummy, the wall only a few yards behind her now.

"Again!" Rhea's voice echoes loudly, as if projected across a deep canyon.

The plague-carrying monster moves implacably toward the dark-haired woman. Lyla is nearly backed against the wall. She looks desperately toward the worried cleric.

Once more Alynn begins the chant to summon the power of Cearn to drive away the creature. At first he feels nothing. Then the buoyancy brought on by the magic starts to surge within him. With growing confidence he recites the ritual words. By its end he feels himself strong with the power of his deity.

The mummy is within a step of Lyla; its shrouded arms are raised and ready to strike. Her back to the wall, the woman watches the undead creature with visible palpitations. Her left hand twitches nervously

Section 69

at her side while the right tenses on her knife.

"By the power of Cearn, begone!" Alynn yells. He strides toward the monster, his ankh extended before him. "Begone!"

At the pronouncement of the command, the tangled strips of musty cloth begin to move as if blown by a strong wind. With the second order the mummy rocks from side to side, barely able to keep its feet.

With obvious effort it turns to face the advancing cleric. Alynn feels the will of the evil force of the creature fighting against Cearn's power. To the man, the air feels as if it has turned into a thick syrup. Each step toward the monster is more difficult. Unseen hands buffet his face and chest.

So suddenly he nearly falls forward, the pressure ends. The mummy is sent tumbling across the temple to slap with audible force against the far wall. Lyla, breathing deeply, rushes to Alynn's side.

She says in a rush, "We had better keep moving. It can return when the power fades."

Feeling empty and drained, Alynn nods in agreement.

Turn to section 75.

69

The door to the right of the altar is made of a dark wood. When Alynn opens it, he notices that the inside of the door has been attacked with a sword or massive claw. There are several gouges and long slashes in the dark wood. Cautiously he peers into the room.

The room is rectangular and runs along the back of the temple. Light from the recently set sun is filtering in through narrow windows set high in the opposite wall. The floor is covered with the smashed pieces of many benches and tables. The charred remains of an altar confirm the priest's suspicion this was once a chapel. A door is visible on the left wall of the room.

Lyla looks over the cleric's shoulder and points toward a sword lying amid the clutter. The tip has been broken off and the blade bent. Both study the large room carefully, but nothing moves. They enter cau-

Section 70

tiously.

A dozen steps into the room, the cleric stops for a few seconds and readies his mace. He knows there is danger here, a threat he should be dreading. Yet the old chapel seems uninhabited. Trying to shrug off the feeling, he continues toward the door on the left wall.

The humans nearly reach the door before the wail begins. It starts as a low moan, growing slowly louder and more menacing. From a groan, the sound changes to a pain-filled cry, loud enough to echo off the wall. As the volume increases, a shape begins to form between the Hero and the doorway.

The shape is outlined in wavery red like the coals of a fire. The door is still visible beyond it. The red halo appears to brighten, and the cry grows louder. The creature takes the form of an old crone. Her eyes are half-closed, and her features are wrinkled and marked by age. Her mouth is open wide, and her arms reach toward them. The cry changes to a shriek filled with hate and despair. The sound is so loud Alynn can feel the head of his mace vibrating. Then the creature begins to drift directly toward the cleric.

If Alynn should cast a Silence spell, turn to section 77.

If Alynn should cast a Spirit Hammer spell, turn to section 74.

If Alynn should fight the monster, turn to section 83.

70

MUMMY
To Hit Alynn: 11   To Be Hit: 9   Hit Points: 10
Damage with Hands: 2 hit points each time it hits, and a chance of disease

When a mummy strikes, it may give its victim a disease. This mummy will transmit a very rapid and virulent form of leprosy. If Alynn is infected, he will immediately lose two points each of Strength and Dexterity. To determine if Alynn is actually infected, roll 3 D6 each time the mummy hits Alynn. If the total is

Section 71, 72

the same as or less than Alynn's value for Constitution, he is not *infected. If the total of the dice is greater than his value for Constitution, he is infected and loses the points.*

If Alynn has chosen the Cure Disease spell, he can cast it after the combat ends. This will also restore any Strength or Dexterity lost from fighting. This spell will not restore any hit points lost, because these are from physical damage, not an effect of the disease.

If Alynn wins the combat, turn to section 75.

If Alynn is defeated, turn to section 29.

71

Roll 3 D6.

If the total is the same as or less than Alynn's Strength value, turn to section 63.

If the total is greater than Alynn's value for Strength he is unable to pull his hand free. Turn to section 66.

If Alynn should fight the mummy, turn to section 70.

If Alynn should cast a Spirit Hammer spell, turn to section 80.

If Alynn should cast a Turn Undead spell, turn to section 68.

72

Its touch is cold. At first the shadows keep their distance. Alynn can feel the mace tear through one, gouts of blackness trailing behind as he pulls it through the creature. It does not scream, but shudders. Then the other touches him. Something is pulled from inside the cleric with a sickly wrenching tear. He fights down a wave of nausea.

Spinning, he swings at the shadow behind him, only to feel the other's frigid touch. His mace grows very heavy. Each swing becomes slower and more difficult than the last.

Section 73

Many more bitterly cold touches rain over his fallen body.

The room seems darker, and the light from his enchantment glows pure white. A rushing sound, like the roar of mountain rapids fills the air, but Alynn is too tired to care. He tries to lift the mace and strike another blow at the darting pools of darkness, but can barely drag it along the floor. The still brightly lit room seems dark to the dying cleric.

The next touch doesn't feel as painfully cold, but almost like a caress. Alynn dimly realizes his body feels distant and weak. He is too tired to care. His world has narrowed to a badly lit corridor with a ragged black silhouette dancing in its center.

The world contracts again, and Alynn welcomes the dive into the darkness. For a moment he feels nothing. Then he slides easily to where there are no more moments.

Turn to section 29.

73

The cleric's eyes are beginning to adjust to the darkness. He guesses they are halfway across the room. Lyla is a deep black form in the darkness beside him. A nervous feeling, more from instinct than from intellect, makes him look back into the center of the ten-foot-wide room. It is hard for the priest to determine if the deeper darkness is really there. How do you see a shadow in the dark? A shadow of what thing, or simply a shadow? His mind conjures up the memory of the black form he encountered two days ago in the Lesser Abbey, and he recalls its freezing touch.

The shadows seem to grow larger as he watches. Their determined flow across the floor changes to a rush. Alynn is barely able to bring up his mace before they are hovering near his head. No light and no bodies, simply two blots of blacker darkness hovering a few feet in front of him. There is no time to chant a spell. It is all the cleric can do to avoid their half-seen thrusts of darkness and keep them at bay with his mace. The shadows' aggressiveness forces the Hero to back

Section 74

away. The dark forms follow.

SHADOWS
To Be Hit (in darkness): 13   To Hit Alynn: 10   Hit Points: 7
Damage: 1 point of Strength permanently lost each time hit

There are two shadows in this room. Shadows can be hit only by magical weapons (a normal mace would automatically miss). If Alynn does not have a magical mace, turn to section 90.

If Alynn's Strength value is lowered to 5 or less, he can do only 1 hit point of damage per hit with the mace. If his Strength is lowered to zero, he is killed.

If Alynn defeats the shadows, his strength is returned to normal; turn to section 81.

If Alynn is killed, turn to section 90.

74

The priest stands amid the echoing wail, poised to throw the small hammer needed for the Spirit Hammer spell. Swiftly, he chants the spell. The cry of the monster seems to echo inside the stone room. It drowns out his voice, and the cleric wonders if a spell can be cast when its invocation cannot be heard. Worried, he hurries to complete the last few words. Still unable to hear himself, Alynn flips the hammer at the glowing figure.

As it spins through the air, the tiny hammer grows larger and becomes less substantial. By the time it reaches the screaming monster, it is as large as the glowing hag's head. It lands with an audible thwack, and the creature's wail rises in intensity. Alynn feels as if the top of his skull is being raised and hot irons dropped inside. His sight fades in and out in reaction to the ululations of its cry. It takes all his concentration to wield the enchanted weapon once more.

Again the hammer hits, and the monster's cry wavers. The cleric's vision clears completely, and he can see that the banshee glows less brightly. Its cry sub-

Section 75

sides to a low moan. His feeling of mystic power fades. Alynn hurries to finish off the undead creature before it can begin a second cry.

BANSHEE
To Hit Alynn: 15   To Be Hit: 11   Hit Points remaining: 4
Damage with Hands: 1 D6-2 and Wail for 3 points of damage

If Alynn does not defeat the banshee in three rounds, it will begin a second cry. At the start of each round after the fourth, the cleric will again be subjected to the banshee's wail. Alynn must roll his Constitution value or less on 3 D6 or receive 3 hit points of damage.

If Alynn defeats the banshee, turn to section 89.

If Alynn is defeated, turn to section 29.

75

Anxious to see what they have gained, Alynn opens the scroll case. Inside is a scroll decorated in the same style as those created in his abbey. This one is dry with age, and the magical parchment is beginning to yellow at its edges. He guesses it was created in the abbey long before the siege. On the scroll are three spells and a warning.

The warning reads:

> Here is the magic of mighty Cearn.
> Use it wisely for you will have but one chance.

The spells listed are Earthquake, Turn Undead, and Heal Wounds. The last two are familiar to Alynn. He has used them before. The first, though, is a powerful enchantment, known only to those much beyond his experience. It, he remembers, creates a fortress-shattering tremor over a small area.

Enter the Scroll of Three Choices on your record sheet. Alynn may use any one of the spells, and then the scroll becomes useless and must be taken off the list. The scroll versions of Turn Undead and Heal Wounds are the same as the spells listed in the Introduction.

Section 75

The sickly odor of the mummy lingers. The putrid scent adds to Alynn's sense of urgency. He knows time is running out. The sunlight has faded almost entirely. In the unlit temple the shadows have grown ominously darker.

"The creature is below us. Can't you feel it?" Lyla asks. There is a distant smile on her face. For a second the woman's eyes seem unfocused. Then, with a self-conscious glance at Alynn, she shakes her head.

"I really do think it is somewhere below us," she finishes in a much different tone while watching the cleric's reaction.

There seems little choice. He has no idea where to look. If Lyla feels the mummy is below them, it may well be. They have to look somewhere, and time is short.

The only routes that might lead downward are through the two doors. Alynn eyes them both, but nothing indicates what waits behind either one. For long moments he waits, unwilling to admit he is hoping for guidance from Rhea. His mind moves in widening circles, finding ever more reasons for despair. A dozen reasons why he should give up the quest race through his mind. Most deal with business unfinished at the abbey, a vine unpruned, a page to be illuminated. Then the image of the abbey as he last saw it washes through his reverie. His mind slams to a painful stop at the scene of the torn bodies of men he has known for over so many years. That vision refuses to fade.

Alynn begins to understand the loneliness he will face forever. For nearly two decades he has had the comradeship of fellow priests of Cearn. They were always a small order. Now he may be the last one left. A black depression threatens to wash over his soul, and the cleric's fingers loosen on the mace. It falls to the end of its strap, scraping the side of his leg. He is too lost in his own dark thoughts to notice.

Minutes pass, and Lyla becomes nervous. She gestures at him, but gets no response. She feels the need to speak, to break the oppressive silence.

"Are you all right?"

The question gives Alynn an anchor with which to

Section 76

drag himself back from the emptiness he now finds inside himself.

Somewhere close by, guarded by perhaps even more horrible creatures, is the Ankh. It appears he can no longer count on Rhea for advice or support. The sun is setting; there is very little time left. Still frowning, the cleric begins to walk, his grip tightening on the mace.

If Alynn should try the door on the left, turn to section 64.

If Alynn should try the door on the right, turn to section 69.

76

Beyond the doors, the two humans find themselves in a tunnel. The walls are crudely cut and supported by unfinished beams. A broken spear lies on the floor a few feet ahead.

"This must be how the forces of the Darklord finally entered the abbey," Alynn guesses.

"It must have been a heroic defense," Lyla comments after a few seconds of surveying the tunnel. "Some of this was cut through solid rock."

"A pity no one will ever know of it," the cleric agrees in a sad voice. As he says it, he realizes they are the only ones who can ever relate the story of the fall of his abbey. With unknown menaces ahead, there is some doubt if they will survive to tell the tale. Absently, he wonders if the Mistwall has yet rolled forward to encompass the Lesser Abbey and its lands.

Fighting depression, Alynn hefts his mace and leads the way down the tunnel. Their only light is Lyla's flickering flame.

A shadow seems to move abnormally on the rough wall.

Alynn freezes, anticipating another attack, but nothing happens. Hardly breathing, both study the rough walls in the dim light. Alynn notices his hand is shaking. After he takes a few deep breaths, it steadies and they continue.

Section 76

The tunnel leads downward. As they walk, dust showers down. Brushing against one of the supporting beams, Alynn notices a piece of wood breaks off easily. The sturdy-looking timbers are rotten with age. They are walking through a centuries-old and hastily built tunnel. Unsummoned and unwelcomed, through the cleric's fatigued mind parade images of him crushed by tons of earth or trapped in a tiny space suffocating on stale air.

Steps hasten to meet the pace of the man's racing heart. His shadow dances ahead of them. Lyla, equally concerned and lost in her own fears, follows. They are nearly running when they emerge into a large chamber.

A horrifying dread is conjured up by brushing through cobwebs. When those strands are as thick as your finger, the fear can only be increased. The grasping threads drag across Alynn's face and tug at his chest and shoulders. Tacky fingers cling chokingly to his arms and neck. The man's startled cry echoes off distant walls. The cleric's heart surges, and he finds himself crouched, ready to fight or flee back down the dark tunnel. He nearly knocks Lyla over as he backs out of the opening.

Perhaps if there were enough light, Alynn tells himself, this room would hold less terror. The red-gold light of the dying flame glints off the intricate webs. A dark blob moves in the murky darkness, then a second.

"Get behind me," Lyla yells.

The cleric hesitates. The woman is armed only with a dagger. Nor is she wearing armor. If the giant spiders are poisonous, even a scratch on her unprotected skin could kill her. As a priest of Cearn, Alynn knows it would be wrong to move behind her. How can a small woman succeed in a battle even he is not sure of winning? It feels wrong.

"Hurry! They are closer."

If Alynn should get behind Lyla, turn to section 98.

If Alynn should stand and fight, turn to section 103.

77

Banshee! the cleric's memory screams at him. Once the abbey had sheltered an old borderer. The soldier had told the tale of a tower far to the south in Tasier. It had once belonged to a necromancer who had allied himself with the Darklord. The soldier had taken part in the final siege of the tower. Orlow himself had broken down the magical barriers to allow his men to storm inside.

On one floor of the tower, there had been a banshee. The borderer had described it as a glowing ghost that screamed. He claimed the monster's wail had killed half his company before Orlow silenced it. Now Alynn faces a similar creature, but with no Orlow to assist him.

Hurriedly he chants the Silence spell. The cry of the monster seems to echo inside the stone room. It drowns out the words of the chant, and the cleric wonders if a spell can be cast when its invocation cannot be heard. With that to worry him, he hurries to complete the last few words.

The sound is so loud that at first he thinks the spell has failed. In the silence, the ringing of his ears is deafening. Then it fades into the eerie stillness. He laughs in relief, but can't hear it. The banshee gazes at the man, shock and frustration on its withered features. Alynn raises his mace and advances on the shimmering monster.

BANSHEE
To Hit Alynn: 15   To Be Hit: 11   Hit Points: 9
Damage with Hands: 1 hit point per attack, 1 attack per round

With its wail silenced, the banshee has only its hands to attack with. Since it is the guardian of this room, it will resist any intruder until destroyed.

If Alynn defeats the banshee, turn to section 89.

If Alynn is killed, turn to section 29.

Section 78

78

The creatures approach boldly. Watching them, Alynn moves away until he has his back to a wall. The shadows leave the walls and glide across the floor. Away from the wall they lose much of their form, becoming clouds of inky blackness from which jagged arms extend. Lyla, he notices, is edging out the door, into the temple. The young woman has her dagger drawn. When she sees both shadows are concerned only with the cleric, she waits in the partly open doorway. Alynn tries to give her a confident smile.

When the shadows are a few steps away from him, the cleric lunges forward and swings his mace. It tears through the substance of the nearest monster and trails wisps of blackness as it continues through. Alynn feels no resistance to the blow, but the form begins to writhe. The cleric notices the head of the mace is cold, so cold a few flecks of frost have formed on it.

The Hero steps back into the corner before the second shadow can react. In the brief respite, Alynn wonders at the Lesser Abbey. Now, facing two of them, he feels almost confident of victory.

Both creatures lunge at him simultaneously. Ducking below their grasping arms, the cleric swings the mace from a crouch. The head tears through the shadow he struck before. With a barely audible whine, it dissolves into tiny black droplets and is gone. The head of the mace now has a thick layer of frost on it.

Confidently Alynn moves toward the remaining monster. He swings the mace back and forth in wide arcs, driving the monster back into the center of the room. It tries to dive past the weapon and strike the cleric with its wavering arms, but instead is struck itself. Keeping the initiative, the Hero begins to swing the heavy mace faster and in tighter arcs. To Alynn the weapon feels feather-light. The shadow collapses under the onslaught, and the mace penetrates its dark form. On the return arc, the mace again slices the shadow, which dissolves into a fine mist. The cleric

Section 79

looks around the room for another foe, but there are no more.

Turn to section 119.

79

The cleric looks around the room for another foe, but he and Lyla are alone. Breathing in deep gasps, he nods to Lyla. The woman is kneeling near the door trying to start a fire with scraps of wood she has shaved from the doorway. She barely notices Alynn. The wood piled loosely in a rusty helmet catches, and they have some light.

Once illuminated, the room seems smaller and less threatening. At the far side is a door, slightly ajar. Alynn hurries over and nudges it open with his mace. For a long moment neither he nor Lyla moves. Then Lyla releases her breath in a long sigh. The cleric realizes he has been holding his breath, too. Looking down at his hand, he notices that it is shaking.

Beyond the doorway is a circular staircase, spiraling its way down into murky darkness. Alynn gestures for his companion to bring the fire forward. In its light they can see a dust-covered floor at the foot of the stairway. Ominously, the dust has been disturbed by numerous footprints, few of them human.

Awkwardly, the follower of Cearn lies down on the floor and peers into the stairwell. With the tip of his mace he sends a flaming scrap of wood spinning down into the room below. As it falls, he leans into the stairwell and glances swiftly around the room below.

It looks deserted.

Alynn finds this a bit hard to believe. In the flickering light he takes another careful look. The hard stone of the floor feels cool against his chest.

"Nothing there," he reassures the woman poised above him.

There are two doors at the far side of the room below and three arched doors on the wall to their left. From the vents in the bottom, Alynn knows those on the left lead to storage closets, probably root cellars or wine storage. He once helped build similar closets at the

Section 79

Lesser Abbey. The plans they used were old, perhaps drawn from the memory of these closets.

The doors on the far wall are set side by side. Even from twenty feet away, Alynn can see that the stone around each door frame is a lighter gray than the rest of the room and the mortar cruder and rougher. The doors have been built recently. Different runes or symbols appear to be inscribed in each door.

Swinging his legs onto the steps, Alynn leads the way down. Only when they are standing before the two doors does he accept that the room holds no new menace. Then he reads the inscription burned into the heavy wooden panels.

The messages are quite simple. They are in runes that were common only a few centuries earlier and that any cleric of Cearn would still know. The inscription on the left-hand door read:

> Ye who follow Cearn shall know your true reward.
> Enter here and forsake any other path.

On the other door, Alynn reads a different inscription:

> Ye who know the might of the Darklord and would serve him, choose only this, his way.

For a long moment the two look at the inscriptions.

"They were probably put here after the Greater Abbey fell," Lyla points out. "That means they are the work of the Darklord. The Darklord is also the Lord of Lies," Lyla adds.

"But if they are from before, they might have been a test for guests. If so, the Darklord's door is trapped. Or the Darklord may have added the second door because the first was enchanted during the siege to keep his minions out."

"Or they were erected by the Darklord to ensure the death of anyone who survived the attack and returned to this abbey."

"Or they both might be trapped," Alynn ended in low tones, wishing he would hear from Rhea again and wondering why he has not. There seemed no pattern to the voice appearing.

They continue to stare at the two doors. Then a flicker forces their decision. The light is failing. They

Section 80

have to choose now or do so in the dark.

Only a dim red glow from the torch remains when Alynn makes his decision. They must continue, and that means either going through one of these doors or going back to try the other door to the right of the altar.

If Alynn should go through the left-hand door, turn to section 112.

If Alynn should go through the right-hand door, turn to section 84.

If Alynn should go back into the temple and go through the door to the right of the altar, turn to section 69.

80

The mummy advances slowly. The arms extend forward. After a few steps Alynn sees the creature is moving toward Lyla, not him. The woman has drawn her knife. She darts the cleric a questioning glance.

In backing away, they have been separated by several steps. The mummy is moving with surprising speed despite its shuffling walk. The green emanating from its face is growing brighter. If Alynn is to stop it from reaching Lyla, he knows he must act now.

Hurrying through the chant, Alynn slips the scroll case into his pocket and digs for the small hammer, which is needed to bring the Spirit Hammer into being. The words of the battle spell are harsh and grating. Even before the spell is completed, the mummy turns and moves toward the cleric. It is only a few steps away when he completes the last phrase and flips the hammer at the advancing monster.

The tiny wooden hammer seems to burst apart in a flash of yellow light. The light forms itself into a glowing hammer half Alynn's height. It smashes into the shrouded corpse with an audible impact.

The creature staggers under the blow. Sweat lines Alynn's lip as he concentrates on striking again with his enchanted weapon. The wavering shape of the hammer clarifies and swings once more into the undead creature's chest. The force of the blow drives the

Section 81

mummy backward. Before it can recover, Alynn rushes forward and smashes into it with his mace. The monster crumples into a pile of dirty rags and dry bones.

Turn to section 75.

81

In the stygian darkness the creatures approach boldly. Watching the black shapes, barely visible in the unlit room, Alynn hurriedly moves until he has his back to a wall. The shadows leave the walls and glide across the floor. As they approach, the shadows become visible as clouds of inky blackness from which arms extend. Sometimes they seem to fade from the worried Hero's sight entirely. Each time he is able to discern their shape, they are closer.

When the shadows are a few steps away, the cleric steps quickly forward and swings his mace. It tears through the substance of one monster and drags away wisps of blackness as he pulls it through. Alynn feels no resistance to the mace, but the form ahead of him writhes. As it passes near him, the cleric notices frost forming on the metal head of the mace. The handle feels bitingly cold even through his leather gloves.

The Hero steps back into a corner before the second shadow can react. In the brief respite, Alynn wonders at the dread one of these conjured monsters created in him at the Lesser Abbey. Now, facing two of them, he is almost confident of victory.

A darker part of the darkness lashes out at his side. Its touch is cold. Then out of the blackness over his head the other shadow touches him. Something is pulled from inside the cleric with a sickly wrenching tear. He fights down a wave of nausea and flails out with his mace. The shadows are driven away, but Alynn leans his back against the wall, sucking in air with painful gasps.

Both creatures lunge at him simultaneously. He sees them as a greater blackness against the room's darkness. Ducking below their grasping arms, the cleric swings the mace while crouched. The head tears through the shadow he struck before, and with a barely

Section 82, 83

audible whine it dissolves into tiny black droplets and is gone. The head of the mace is coated with a thin layer of frost.

A dim light fills the room as Lyla opens the door to the temple. The last rays of sunset bounce red into the corridor. A few steps ahead of him the cleric sees the dark form of the other shadow. Confidently Alynn moves toward the second monster. He swings the mace back and forth in wide arcs, driving the monster back into the center of the room. It tries to get past the weapon to strike the cleric with its waving arms, but instead is struck itself. Keeping the initiative, the Hero begins to swing the heavy mace faster and in tighter arcs. Somehow the weapon feels feather-light. The shadow collapses under the onslaught, and the mace penetrates its dark form. On the return arc the mace slices through the shadow once more and the monster dissolves into a fine mist.

Turn to section 79.

82

"Down," Alynn yells, shoving the woman forward. She screams as she tumbles to the floor near the table with the coins. He hears the hum of the bow at the same instant the bolt slams him against the wall.

Glancing off his arm and ramming through the chain mail on his chest, the bolt tears into the muscles over his heart. If he had been standing at a different angle, the cleric realizes in those numb instants before the pain begins, his quest would be over. Then he looks down at the wound as it starts to throb.

Roll 1 D6 to determine the damage done by the crossbow. If Alynn is killed by the bolt, turn to section 96.

If Alynn survives the attack, turn to section 87.

83

BANSHEE
To Hit Alynn: 15   To Be Hit: 11   Hit Points: 9
Damage with Hands: 1 D6-2 and Wail

Section 84, 85

In addition to its normal attack, the banshee attacks with its wail. As part of each round of its attack the banshee wails. Each round Alynn must roll his Constitution value or less on 3 D6 or receive 3 hit points of damage.

If Alynn defeats the banshee, turn to section 92.

If Alynn is killed, turn to section 29.

84

As the light flickers out, Alynn pushes open the right-hand door. The room beyond appears empty. Tall windows set high in the wall allow in starlight. In the center of the room is a jagged hole in the floor. Around the hole are piles of rock and dirt.

Stepping through the door, Alynn tenses. At first he feels nothing.

"You're glowing," Lyla blurts out.

The cleric looks down and sees that a gentle red light is playing over his robes. Barely visible, even in only starlight, the color dances over his rope and then fades.

"Good choice," Lyla compliments the cleric as she follows him through the right doorway. Alynn sees the same light play over her sleek form and fade gently away.

Turn to section 76.

85

There is little doubt in Alynn's mind as to what this creature is. The Lesser Abbey had once been attacked by a powerful necromancer. Instead of summoning a horde as the Darklord would have done, that necromancer had called a single creature much like this one. It had preyed on the brothers for several days until the abbot was able to turn and then destroy it. Alynn had only seen the other monster from across a courtyard, but a creature as ungodly as a wraith makes a permanent impression.

Backing away from the slowly advancing claws,

Section 85

Alynn pulls the scroll from its silver case. Half afraid to take his eyes off the approaching undead, he searches the parchment. The words are written in elegant letters. Hurriedly he holds the scroll so he can read it and watch the wraith at the same time. Even as he reads the words needed to drive the monster back, Alynn can sense its ravenous hunger. A hunger not for his flesh, but to absorb and destroy his otherwise immortal soul. For a brief instant he senses the anguish in the insatiable emptiness approaching him. His heartbeat hammers in his chest, and the cleric nearly skips an entire line of the invocation.

Fighting down panic, the man forces himself to carefully complete the spell. As he speaks the last lines, Cearn's power surges up to soothe him.

"Begone in the name of Cearn!" the cleric commands the form floating only a few feet ahead of him. The wraith slows with its clawed hands raised, but does not retreat. Fear and doubt tear at the concentration Alynn needs to maintain the spell he has just read.

"Begone!" he yells almost frantically.

The hovering creature smiles a most horrible and hungry smile. It moves a few inches closer.

Forcing himself to be calm, the priest takes a hesitant step forward and once more orders the undead monster to depart.

This time it retreats, though only the slightest fraction of a step. This reaction gives the cleric courage. It can be driven off. He drops the now useless parchment and grips his Ankh in both hands. The mace dangles from his wrist, hitting his stomach, but he doesn't even notice its weight.

"Begone, foul monster," Alynn orders in even tones. Then he steps forward, thrusting his double Ankh into the apparition's fanged face. If he does not drive it off, the cleric will have stepped into the arms of the soul eater.

The glowing form cringes visibly as it pulls back from the man and his holy symbol. The cleric takes another step forward, and the wraith retreats, angry and frustrated. Pulling himself into his most commanding pose, Alynn once orders the monster to return to the

Section 86

plane from which it came.

The glowing form folds into itself and begins to grow smaller. Before the cleric can react, all that remains is a glowing point of foul green light throbbing in the center of the small corridor. Alynn reaches forward with his double Ankh and touches the glow. A whine, pitched so high it is more felt than heard, echoes in the narrow chamber and then it is gone.

For seconds Alynn is unable to move. His left leg begins to quiver uncontrollably as he realizes the gravity of the danger he has just faced. He takes a step and then stumbles forward to lean against the wall. The Ankh snags the edge of a large pocket when he tries to put it away with trembling hands. Sweat he had not noticed before runs down his neck and spine.

Remove the scroll from your list of magical items on the record sheet.

Turn to section 88.

86

Calming himself, the cleric notices a deeper groove in the stone blocks running parallel to the floor at waist level. Bending lower, he pushes again, and the waist-high panel moves easily. A rush of cool air beckons him forward. Crouching low, the cleric scuttles into the room ahead.

Seeing the way clear, Lyla hurries past the stone altar and follows Allyn through the low opening. Behind them the altar starts to cool. By the time they push the panel closed, the glow has faded.

Lyla is carrying the stub of a candle she has snatched off a table. The heat of the altar has softened it, and it droops awkwardly. She sparks it to light quickly with her flint. Crouched, ready to meet an attack, Alynn studies the faintly illuminated room.

The room is empty. Scuffed footprints on the dusty floor warn of potential danger, but no threat appears to lurk in the shadowy corners. After the menace of the other rooms they have passed through, Alynn finds this

Section 87

a bit hard to believe. In the flickering light he looks carefully around once more.

"Nothing," he reassures Lyla.

There are two doors at the far side and three arched doors on the wall to their left. From the vents at the bottom, Alynn knows those on the left lead to closets, likely root cellars or wine storage. He once helped build similar closets along at the Lesser Abbey. They had used old plans, perhaps drawn from the memory of these closets. Rhea had spoken of a cavern. It is unlikely there will be any route down through them.

The doors on the far wall are set side by side. Even from twenty feet away, Alynn can see they have been recently added. The stone around each door frame is lighter in color and the mortar is cruder and rougher than that in the rest of the wall. Different runes or symbols appear to be inscribed in each door.

The inscriptions are burned into the heavy wooden doors. From dust gathered in their grooves, Alynn guesses they were inscribed a long time ago.

Turn to section 79.

87

The wound looks serious. The crossbow bolt has dug a path along his chest and wedged itself in the chain mail over his heart. Blood pours from the wound. Lyla hurries over and tears another long strip from the hem of her robe. Absently, through a haze of pain, Alynn notices the robe has become improperly short. He considers the place and their quest, and the thought amuses him. He nearly passes out when Lyla pulls the chainmail byrnie off over his head. Her hands feel soothing as she binds the jagged tear.

Within a few minutes the bleeding stops completely, and the pain settles down to an annoying throb. A few minutes later the cleric finds he can almost stand. Lyla helps him carefully put on what is left of the armor. Regaining his mace, Alynn leads the way across the room.

Turn to section 91.

Section 88

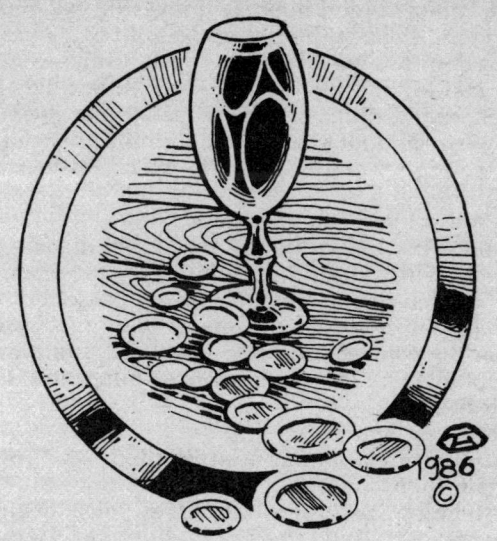

88

Alynn leans on a table, his legs barely able to support him after the tension of his life-and-death struggle. The world seems to rock from side to side; only the image of the hungry wraith remains steady. Lyla, perhaps sensing his shock, says nothing to him as she crawls from under a table and pulls herself to her feet. Once the world has steadied itself, the cleric pulls himself upright, his eyes searching the room for any sign of another threat. He is amazed instead to see the dark-haired woman turn her back and begin sweeping the coins off the table into a pouch.

"Should you do that?" he asks. "They could be cursed."

"Not *money*," the Gama answers, pronouncing the word as if it has special meaning. The cleric realizes that to her it probably does. He knows nothing of the Gamas except that they are wandering merchants,

Section 88

though rumors brand them as thieves or worse. After a few more seconds the last of the gold coins has disappeared into a pouch. The pouch vanishes somewhere inside her dress. In another place he might have enjoyed speculating on where the woman was concealing things under her revealing robe. Instead, the cleric wonders why he has not heard from Rhea for so long.

"Because I've been very busy."

Alynn is instantly relieved to hear her distant voice and is as swiftly angry with himself for the reaction.

"Where have you been?" Alynn tries to sound stern.

"There have been...powers, powers that made it hard for me contact you," Rhea explains, sounding almost apologetic. The cleric realizes her voice is firm and clear again.

"Was it the wraith?"

"Hardly." Rhea sounds a bit insulted.

"What, then?"

"Just below, in...a cavern." Her voice begins to fade in and out. "Evil...powers...the gate." Her voice is obscured by a sound similar to parchment being crumpled near his ear. The noise soon rises to a roar like that of a great waterfall. The follower of Cearn strains to hear Rhea's voice, but in seconds even the roar of sound fades.

Alynn finds it difficult not to feel abandoned. Whatever the voice is—whether it really exists or not—it was at its urging he began this quest. He who after his years as a soldier had been content to lead the sedate life of a priest of Cearn. Now, when he is deep inside the ruins of a haunted abbey, he can't even depend on it. Resentment, fueled by adrenaline left from the battle, wells up. For a moment he is lost to the anger.

"I said, hadn't we better keep moving?" Lyla is demanding. "Are you all right? Can you hear me?"

"Keep going," Alynn agrees self-consciously, as he moves toward the short corridor the wraith had inhabited. This time it is empty.

The door on the far end of the corridor is unlocked. Beyond it, in the faint light, Alynn sees the remains of a small altar, only knee high and a foot square. What-

Section 88

ever once stood on it has been long since removed. Behind it is only a frustratingly solid-looking wall. The cleric stands and stares at the masonry, his mind refusing to accept this next obstruction.

"The Darklord wouldn't have set anything as powerful as a specter to guard an empty altar," Lyla points out.

Alynn just stares, torn between the last of his anger at Rhea and despair of recovering the Ankh in time.

For nearly a minute Lyla waits for the cleric to act. His angry expression and unfocused eyes worry her. The priest stands unmoving ten feet short of the dead end. The dark-haired woman begins to fear he has been charmed by some trap in the hallway or on the altar. Hesitantly she looks around the corridor, but can find no sign of a symbol.

"Alynn, wake up!" she demands loudly, standing close to him.

From beyond a familiar roaring in his head, a second voice joins in. "Cleric, it is time to act. I command it!"

Slowly, painfully, the lonely, fatigued man forces his thoughts through the anger. Depression tries to drain him, but then, with a physical shudder, Alynn ends the introspection.

"The Darklord wouldn't have set a specter to guard an empty altar," Lyla repeats. "There has to be a way out, a hidden door or panel."

Reluctant to speak, Alynn steps past the altar and begins searching the wall for a secret opening. The sensation of warmth on the back of his neck and Lyla's gasp warn him of the new danger.

Behind him, the altar now glows red from intense heat. Some magical force is causing the stones to grow hotter even as they watch. Portions of the altar gleam white. Already Alynn can feel the cloth of his robe warming to a painful level. Hurriedly the cleric pushes on the wall. It is as unmovable as it appeared. He knows he has only a few seconds to find the switch that will open the secret door before the heat becomes unbearable. Wisps of smoke begin to drift up from the back of his robe. Sweat makes his eyes sting.

Turn to section 113.

Section 89

89

Lyla approaches with a concerned look. She appears to have withstood or entirely avoided the creature's scream. Her lips are moving, but the cleric cannot hear her. Frustrated, he gestures at his ears. Both wait, watching for any new danger, while the ringing in Alynn's ears diminishes enough so that they can talk.

"It is late," Lyla speaks slowly to ensure he can hear her. She gestures toward the reddening rays of the sunlight entering through the narrow windows.

"How is it you are not hurt?" the cleric asks.

Lyla answers by putting her fingers in her ears and shrugging. Alynn shakes his head ruefully.

"We may as well get going," he comments, leading the way toward the door on the west wall.

Standing in front of the door, both are surprised to find it open about an inch. Alynn tries to look into the next room without moving it farther, but the edge of the door does not quite clear the jamb. The floor near the door shows a wedge shape plainly visible in the thick dust. Someone has used the door recently.

"It looks almost too inviting," Alynn observes, remembering all of the monsters they have found beyond other doorways. "Maybe a trap?"

"A banshee wouldn't need to open a door."

"Would the Darklord?"

"Let's hope we don't find out."

"Maybe I can push it open just a crack," the priest volunteers.

"We have to keep going, no matter what is there," Lyla remarks pointedly. "Time is running out."

Crouching low and gesturing his companion to one side, Alynn nudges the door open a few inches farther.

Nothing. No sound or movement.

He pushes the door open a few more inches.

Still no reaction. Much of the next room is visible now. It is the same width as the one they are in, but much shorter. Another door is clearly visible against the wall.

Alynn waves the head of the mace through the door-

Section 90

way. No skeletal or rotting hand attacks. He uses the mace to shove open the door the rest of the way. The walls of the room are lined with tables. On one table several small piles of gold and silver coins are visible. Alynn hears a sudden intake of breath behind him.

Turning, he sees Lyla looking past his shoulder at the coins. She is staring at them with obvious fascination.

"Perhaps we had better move on," he comments in low tones. She nods her head in emphatic agreement. Startled and a bit amused at his companion's greed, the cleric walks into the empty room. Lyla begins to push past him just as he notices the crossbow fastened to a table along the wall to his left. It is pointed directly at him.

Glancing down, he sees Lyla to his left. Her foot is breaking the cord stretched across the floor. The far end of the cord is wrapped around the trigger of the crossbow.

Roll 3 D6.

If the total is the same as or less than Alynn's value for Dexterity, turn to section 110.

If the total is greater than Alynn's value for Dexterity, turn to section 82.

90

There are many kinds of cold. Some types come from within and bring a shudder to every part of the body. At first the shadows keep their distance. Then Alynn feels the mace tear into one, gouts of blackness trailing behind as he pulls it through the creature. It does not scream, but seems to shrink into itself. Then the other touches him from behind. They are frighteningly quick. Something is pulled from inside him with a sickly wrenching tear. The cleric fights down a wave of nausea, and a rush of cold seems to spread out in every direction from the center of his body.

Spinning, he swings at the shadow behind him, only to feel the frigid touch of the first. His mace feels very heavy. Just to lift it becomes a challenge. Each swing

Section 91

seems slower and more difficult than the last.

Many more bitterly cold touches follow, each accompanied by the same sickly wrench, as something is rent from the cleric.

The room seems even darker. He can't see the shadows or Lyla at all. Maybe he hears her scream, but it doesn't seem to matter anymore. A rushing sound louder than the roar of mountain rapids fills the air, but Alynn is too tired to care. He tries to lift the mace and strike another blow at the pools of darkness hanging about him, but he can barely drag it across the floor.

The next touch doesn't feel as painfully cold; it hardly feels like anything at all. Alynn dimly realizes his body seems distant and weak. So distant this sensation means nothing to him. He is simply too tired to care. The world has narrowed to a badly lit tunnel with a ragged black silhouette mocking him from its center.

Then the tunnel closes, and Alynn welcomes the dive into a darkness blacker than the shadows. For a moment as he falls the cleric regrets he has failed. Then he slides easily to where there are no more moments.

Turn to section 29.

91

Alynn glances around the room, but sees no other traps. Moving over to the crossbow, he notices there is no rust on the crosspiece. Nor is the leather dry or the wood decayed. This weapon has been placed there recently. He wonders if the Darklord is aware of his quest. With a renewed sense of urgency the follower of Cearn rushes to the door on the west wall of the room. He pulls it toward him. Behind him, he can hear the sound of coins being scooped off the table.

The door opens onto a small corridor. It is barely five feet long, four feet wide, and just tall enough for a man to stand in upright. Bursting through the doorway is a translucent shape. It is the size of a man, but only a horrible parody of a human being. The creature has no mouth, just a fanged gash. Behind the fangs is a velvety darkness. Its eyes glow with a mad yellow light, and they scream of a terrible hunger. Claw-tipped

Section 92, 93

fingers grab for the cleric's throat. Alynn lurches back and scrambles out of the creature's reach.

If Alynn should cast a Turn Undead spell, turn to section 101.

If Alynn should cast a Light spell, turn to section 95.

If Alynn should cast the Turn Undead spell from the scroll, turn to section 85.

If Alynn should fight the monster, turn to section 93.

92

The banshee's keening wail echoes off the stone walls. Alynn feels as if the top of his skull is being raised and hot irons dropped inside. His vision fades and sharpens with the ululations of its cry. It takes all his concentration to wield his mace against the glowing figure wavering ahead of him. Whenever the iron head of the weapon strikes the creature, its cry becomes even more piercing than before. Dust rattles off the walls and ceiling. Another blow and its cry wavers for a few seconds, then begins again. Encouraged, the cleric strikes once more. The wavering scream drops to a pitiful moan.

Even as the priest's vision clears, the banshee begins to fade from sight. There is a look of terrible agony and frustration on its withered features. With a final blow from the mace, it disappears entirely.

Alynn staggers against the wall, dizzy and drained. His ears continue to ring for several minutes.

Turn to section 89.

93

WRAITH
To hit Alynn: 10   To Be Hit: 13   Hit Points: 9
Damage with Claws and Fangs: 1 D6 per round

Each time the wraith succeeds in hitting Alynn with its claws, roll 3 D6.

If the total is the same as or less than Alynn's value for Wisdom, nothing is lost. If the total is greater than

Section 94, 95

Alynn's Wisdom value, he will take an additional 1 D6 of damage from the wraith's soul drain.

A wraith exists on both the plane of evil and the plane of Earth. Because of this, it can be harmed only by magic and enchanted weapons. If Alynn has an enchanted mace, roll the combat in the normal manner. If he does not, he cannot harm the creature and will be defeated.

If Alynn defeats the wraith, turn to section 102.

If Alynn is killed, turn to section 29.

94

Slipping the scroll into his pocket, Alynn draws his mace. The vulture-demon is materializing too quickly to allow him time to complete a spell. Alynn raises his mace and watches the demon appear amid glittering sparks.

VULTURE-DEMON
To Hit Alynn: 10   To Be Hit: 13   Hit Points: 11
Damage from Claws: 1 D6; from Teeth: 1 D6

The vulture-demon will attack twice each round, once with claws and once with teeth. It has been sent to kill whomever it finds near the Demon Gate and then to recover the Ankh. It cannot return to its own plane until the Ankh is returned. It will fight until destroyed.

Because Alynn is ready and waiting for it to appear, he gets two attacks before the melee. This means you will roll three times for Alynn before you roll the demon. After this, proceed normally.

If Alynn defeats the vulture-demon, turn to section 120.

If Alynn is killed, turn to section 29.

95

The wraith drifts toward the retreating cleric. Smaller than a man, it floats relentlessly forward, ignoring everything but its intended victim. Stumbling back-

Section 95

ward past chairs and tables, the cleric feels his heart racing as the figure moves relentlessly closer. He can feel its hunger, see the terrible need behind its glowing eyes. Inside the manlike form is a void. Death and its own evil have doomed the creature to be forever incomplete. By its very nature the undead monster is forced to tear the spirit from others in a futile attempt to fill its own emptiness. As the creature moves slowly toward him, sweat runs down Alynn's forehead, threatening to blind him. He is afraid to wipe his forehead and take the risk of covering his eyes. The cleric must not lose sight of the advancing wraith for even a few seconds.

Alynn remembers years earlier when an evil priest attacked the Lesser Abbey. He had summoned only one powerful creature to make the attack, not hordes such as those the Darklord unleashed. Then it had been a wraith similar to this one. For days the ever hungry monster had preyed on the brothers, until the abbot himself had helped to trap and destroy it. Three more brothers had died in that final battle. Now the cleric faces such a creature alone.

Alynn realizes he needs an edge. In a straight battle of strength, a lone man has little chance. He begins to chant the Light spell.

It is one of the simplest and most basic of invocations, one taught every novice upon his admission to the abbey. For a long, lonely second Alynn remembers there is no longer a Lesser Abbey, just a corpse-strewn ruin. He almost loses the spell, but then his new hatred for all undead, and the lord they serve, steadies his words.

The head of his mace begins to glow, not with the sickly greens or infected reds of evil, but with the clean brightness of daylight.

The room is filled with light as the cleric completes the spell, light brighter than this place has seen in a century. Outlined in it are the hovering menace of the wraith and a cleric in tattered chain mail with his mace raised and ready. In the shadow of a table near the corner is the crouching form of a woman.

The light grows brighter, and the wraith hesitates.

Section 96, 97

It is clearly uncomfortable, sheltering its face with a clawed hand. Then it continues its advance, hurrying now to eliminate the discomfort of the light. Unfortunately, Alynn knows, the only way to end the continual Light spell is to kill the caster. He has guaranteed the monster will attack until one of them perishes.

WRAITH

To Hit Alynn (in daylight): 12   To Be Hit (magic weapons only and in daylight): 11   Hit Points: 10
Damage: With Claws and Fangs 1 D6 per round

Each time the wraith succeeds in hitting Alynn with its claws, roll 3 D6. If the total is the same as or less than Alynn's Wisdom value, he will take an additional 1 D6 of damage from the wraith's soul drain.

A wraith exists on both the plane of evil and the plane of Earth. Because of this, it can be harmed only by magic and enchanted weapons. If Alynn has an enchanted (+1 or +2) mace, roll the combat in the normal manner. If he does not, he cannot harm the creature and will be defeated (turn to section 29).

If Alynn defeats the wraith, turn to section 88.

If Alynn is killed, turn to section 29.

96

The dizziness comes before the pain. Blood is flowing from the wound in throbbing surges. Alynn raises a hand to his chest, but cannot stanch the flow of blood. The mace slips out of his numb fingers and thumps onto the floor, sounding very distant. The thud of his own collapse is meaningless. Then a pain-filled crimson world disappears in a rush of darkness.

Turn to section 29.

97

The wall he is searching also begins to warm from the intense heat emanating from the altar. Thicker smoke begins to drift off the back of Alynn's robe, and

Section 98

the chain mail stings his back like whip wounds even through the robe below it. Frantically the cleric pushes on every stone and brick in front of him. His eyes search for some hint of a lever or button. Waves of heat are starting to make vision difficult, and sweat pours over his eyes. When he raises an arm to wipe them clear, he notices that his sleeve is already singed.

Alynn has received 3 hit points of damage from the heat. Subtract this from his total on the record sheet.

If Alynn still lives, turn to section 100.

If Alynn is killed by the heat, turn to section 8.

98

"Be careful," Alynn cautions as he steps back from the end of the tunnel. "You can't fight giant spiders with a dagger."

Standing behind her, ready to jump to her defense, he can't see the lithe woman smile knowingly in the half-light. The flame of her candle dims slightly when she touches it to the nearest strand of the web. The web dances as the half-seen spiders rush toward her. Bracing himself to dash forward, the cleric watches the eight-legged monsters skitter across their webs. Their black carapaces glisten, and those hairy legs seem almost impossibly thin to be supporting their foot-wide bodies. When the giant insects are almost close enough to strike, the flame flares and races up the web. Immediately the room fills with flame.

A thick smoke rolls into the top of the tunnel, and the cleric crouches to avoid it. The air is filled with an odor reminding Alynn of burning animal fat dripping onto a cookfire. The two spiders try to escape the flames by retreating up the web but before they can reach the top they are overtaken by the racing fire. The spiders emit a piping shriek as the hair on their legs bursts into flame. A third arachnid falls from somewhere above Lyla to land writhing at her feet. The woman takes a quick step backward and then smiles, pleased, as the last of the web falls burning onto the floor of the chamber. Alynn looks around for any sign of the Demon

Section 99

Gate while the flames last. In less than a minute, the only remnant of the webs or spiders is smoke drifting around three charred husks.

Turn to section 99.

99

The spiders defeated, the couple cautiously enter the again dark chamber. Feeling her way along the wall, Lyla finds a torch lying on the floor below the ceiling from which the webs hung, perhaps dropped by a previous victim. It has remained untouched. At the sound of flint on steel Alynn freezes. Before he can

Section 99

move, Lyla lights the torch. After the complete darkness of the underground chamber, the light from the single torch seems almost uncomfortably bright.

The chamber is el-shaped. They have entered on the shorter arm. The walls are smooth, as if worn by water, but the ceiling is studded with stalactites. When he reaches the corner, Alynn can see light under a doorway at the far end of the el. As they approach the door, both can hear a voice chanting.

There appears to be no lock on the door. Alynn grips the rotted rope that serves as a handle and pulls gently. The door moves a fraction of an inch and then begins to grind. The cleric lets go as if the rope were scalding him. What if the chanter behind noticed the movement or heard the ancient hinges screech?

The muffled voice beyond continues to chant in an unfamiliar language. For several breaths neither Lyla nor Alynn moves. Both are aware that beyond could be the Demon Gate. If so, the voice is likely that of the Darklord himself. The thought of facing the legendary villain is daunting. The cleric cannot conceive of joining combat with mankind's centuries-old enemy.

With a determined gesture, Alynn orders the woman to stand clear of the door. Hoping to remain undetected for as long as possible, he begins to draw the door open silently and slowly. Neither human dares even to draw a breath. The eerie singsong chant grows louder as the edge of the door pulls free of the frame. Alynn almost relaxes, allowing himself to believe the old door can be opened smoothly. When he pulls again, there is little resistance. The greatest danger is that the door will open too quickly. His arm is tense from the strain as he tries to pull the door smoothly and very slowly open. Lyla's eyes jump from the slowly opening door to the figure of a man kneeling at the far side of the well-lit room beyond.

Roll 3 D6.

If the total is the same as or less than Alynn's value for Dexterity, turn to section 111.

If the total is greater than Alynn's Dexterity value, turn to section 138.

Section 100, 101

100

As the skin on Alynn's back and legs begins to char, Lyla screams. The cleric is half blinded by the heat and tormented by the pain; his mind races wildly.

If Alynn should continue to search for the opening, turn to section 113.

If Alynn should retreat into the corridor and try a different route, turn to section 69.

101

There is little doubt in Alynn's mind as to what this creature is. Three years earlier the Lesser Abbey of Cearn had been attacked by a powerful necromancer. Instead of summoning a horde, as the Darklord would have done, the necromancer had summoned a creature much like this one. It had preyed on the brothers for several days until the abbot was able to turn and then destroy it. Alynn had only seen the other monster from across a courtyard, but a thing as ungodly as a wraith makes a permanent impression.

Backing away with his eyes locked on the slowly advancing claws, Alynn begins the Turn Undead chant. Even as he speaks the words needed to drive the monster back, he can sense its ravenous hunger. A hunger not for his flesh, but to take and destroy his otherwise immortal soul. For a brief instant he senses the anguish in the insatiable emptiness of the evil creature approaching him. His heartbeat hammers in his chest, and the cleric nearly mispronounces a key word while dodging a flailing claw.

Fighting down the panic, the man forces himself to carefully complete the invocation. When he yells out the last defiant words, the power of Cearn surges through his body to soothe him.

"Begone in the name of Cearn!" the cleric commands the form floating only a few feet ahead of him. The wraith slows, but does not retreat. Fear and doubt tear at the concentration Alynn needs to maintain the spell.

Section 102

"Begone!" the cleric yells almost frantically.

The hovering creature smiles a most horrible and hungry smile. It edges a few more inches toward him.

Forcing himself to be calm, the priest takes a hesitant step forward and once more orders the undead monster to depart.

This time it retreats, though only the slightest fraction of a step. This reaction gives the cleric confidence. The wraith can be driven off.

"Begone, foul monster," Alynn orders in even tones. This time he steps forward, thrusting his double Ankh into the apparition's fanged face. If he does not drive it off, the man has stepped into the waiting arms of the soul eater.

The glowing form cringes visibly as it pulls back to avoid being touched by the holy symbol. Another step forward and the wraith retreats, angry and frustrated. The cleric's voice wavers with nervous laughter as he orders the monster to return to the plane from which it came. He thrusts the double Ankh into its cloudy silhouette.

The glowing form folds into itself and begins to grow smaller. Before the cleric can react, all that remains is a glowing point of foul green light throbbing in the center of the small corridor. Alynn reaches forward with his double Ankh and touches it. A whine, pitched so high it is more felt than heard, echoes in the narrow chamber, and then he is alone.

For seconds the cleric is unable to move. His legs feel weak as he begins to comprehend the horror he has just defeated. He walks a few steps, but his left leg begins to shake so badly he can only lean against the wall. The Ankh snags on the edge of a large pocket and tears the fabric when his trembling hand tries to pull it away. Sweat he had not noticed before runs down the back of his neck and spine.

Turn to section 88.

102

The wraith advances toward the cleric. He can feel its hunger, see the terrible need behind its glowing eyes. Inside the manlike form is a void. Death and its

Section 102

own evil have doomed the creature to be ever incomplete and driven to tear the spirit from others in a futile attempt to fill its own emptiness. Alynn senses the horror and anguish threatening his otherwise immortal soul. Sweat begins to blind him, and his grip on the mace grows slippery.

The cleric remembers three years before when an evil necromancer attacked the Lesser Abbey. The memory is interrupted by a rising surge of loneliness and loss. There no longer is a Lesser Abbey. Just ruins strewn with the corpses of his friends and brothers. Three years earlier, only one creature had been summoned, not hordes such as the Darklord had unleashed. That had been a wraith much like the one now approaching. For days the monster had preyed on the brothers, until the abbot himself had helped to trap and destroy it. Three more brothers had died in the final battle. Now Alynn faced another such creature alone.

When Alynn can retreat no farther, he raises his mace high over one shoulder. Ignoring the weapon, the wraith steadily advances. Its claws reach forward, and the fanged hole where a man would have a mouth gapes expectantly. Driven by the sheer horror of the monster, Alynn takes a half-step forward and strikes.

The mace leaves a trail of wispy blackness where it rips through the hovering apparition. The jagged gap of its mouth opens wider in silent protest. The cleric swings again and feels the pain of ephemeral but effective claws raking his forearm. By the time the mace has completed its second arc, Alynn can feel a slippery warmth trickling down his right arm.

The wraith rushes at the cleric, trying to get inside the effective range of the mace. Its hideous parody of a face looms inches before the cleric's eyes. Crouching, Alynn slips under its deadly embrace. Spinning on one heel, he prepares to strike again.

The undead creature spins, raging, and Alynn feels the pain as its fangs find the gap left in his armor by the skeletal harpy. The teeth plunge into his shoulder. He feels pain on a level far deeper than ordinary sensation as the monster tries to tear away a portion of his

Section 103

soul. Time loses it relevance as they battle on for higher stakes than life. The physical battle forgotten, the man gathers into himself and resists the pull of the void. A tiny part of him seems to be torn loose and pulled into the emptiness. He feels a pain that has no location; it is just an awareness of agony. The suction of the void increases, and Alynn fights to maintain the integrity of his own being. The pressure grows until it seems just short of unbearable. He can feel portions of his soul begin to leave him. Then the conflict ends.

With a shock, awareness of the physical battle returns. The wraith has pulled away, its fangs dripping a golden liquid. The monster's frightening hunger seems to have grown even more ravenous. Desperately the cleric swings the mace at the apparition hovering in front of him, weaving a pattern that plunges the iron head through its ephemeral form several times.

Inside, in the jagged gap where a part of him has been lost, he hears the monster scream. On the physical plane, the wraith's glowing form seems to drift apart and then be pulled back in a rush to collapse into the darkness inside itself. Then the hungry darkness, having consumed itself, shrinks first to a point of sickly green light and then to a pulsing spot of velvet black only an inch across. Then the spot surges outward, and the cleric cringes. Before he can move farther, the ball of darkness seems to fold into itself and is gone.

Turn to section 88.

103

SPIDERS
To Be Hit: 12   To Hit Alynn: 11   Hit Points: 9 each
Damage: 1 D6 plus Poison

Each time Alynn is hit by a spider, roll 3 D6.

If the total is less than Alynn's value for Constitution, he receives an additional 1 D6 of damage from poison.

If the total is the same as or greater than Alynn's Constitution value, the poison will have no effect.

There are three spiders. Only one will attack on the

first round, but this spider will drop from above and have the first attack. In the second and later rounds all three will attack.

If Alynn is killed turn to section 109.

If Alynn defeats the spiders, turn to section 98.

104

The cleric of Cearn watches with horror as the sparks coalesce into a floor-to-ceiling rod a few inches in front of him. Before he can focus on the radiant green pole, it bursts apart, throwing sparks in all directions. Too late, he dives for the protection of the door. Each spark ignites the air around it. This blast throws him against the wall. He can feel the skin of his back and legs curl and peel off from the scorching heat.

Looking back, Alynn sees a ten-foot pillar of fire. The waves of heat and the nearly deafening roar send him scuttling along the floor. Dazed, for long moments he is aware of nothing but the excruciating protests from his blistered back. The few remaining strips of his robe feel like whiplashes where they brush against his cracked and brittle flesh.

Through the haze of pain he hears Rhea, her voice unintelligible but urgent. He knows he has to stand up. He must rise and face the Darklord. The Darklord who has already defeated two abbeys of Alynn's brothers, one despite the cleric's earlier efforts. With this renewed awareness of the power he now faces, his determination fades. Barely able to bite back a sob of agony, he drags himself along the wall toward the door.

Suddenly a globe of intensely blue light hovers over the fallen man. Fearing another attack, the cleric cringes. His world has contracted to a sphere of pain, and this new threat promises to only make things worse. He hears himself whimper. A halfhearted swing of the mace does not even reach the glowing figure forming from the light.

The pillar of fire does 3 D6 of damage to Alynn. The cure from the glowing figure does 2 D6 of healing.

Section 105, 106

If Alynn is killed, turn to section 126.

If, including the cure, Alynn survives, turn to section 130.

105

Add a +1 mace to Alynn's list of magical items. He may use this mace in any future combats. See the Introduction on pages 6 and 7 for how to include the bonus for a magical weapon.

Turn to section 61.

106

The cleric is lying in the room where the tunnel enters the abbey.

The floor is both pleasantly substantial and painfully hard. Alynn lies there for several minutes, readjusting to the material world and simply enjoying the normal surroundings. Breathing feels strange, and he has to take several breaths before he trusts his lungs to continue without his supervision. Still somewhat wobbly, he pulls himself to his feet.

It is daylight again. At least one night must have passed since he was pushed through the Gate. Several unlit torches hang on the wall. Taking one, Alynn scrapes his flint on the head of his mace to light it.

The cleric is glad to have the torchlight. Still unsteady, he lowers himself carefully into the tunnel. Cautiously he retraces his steps.

To Alynn's relief, the black-floored room is empty. The Demon Gate, without the Ankh, is just a pattern of runes and lines inscribed on the stone wall. To one side, the scorch mark of Lyla's lightning bolt stands out in contrast on the gray granite. The cleric stands in front of the intricately carved runes, wondering what Rhea meant when she said there was a way to prevent the Gate from ever being used. He knows that as long as the Ankh exists, it can be fitted into the slot, and the Demon Gate can be opened.

Whatever the opportunity is, he tells himself, it is

passing. The cleric wishes he just once on this quest had the time to make a careful decision. But again he must decide quickly and without all the information needed.

"You have what you need." Rhea's voice sounds distant now. Suddenly the roaring returns louder than ever before, and any further advice she might have given is lost.

If Alynn should leave the abbey in pursuit of Lyla, turn to section 122.

If Alynn should stay in the room and use a spell from the mummy's scroll, turn to section 128.

If Alynn should use his mace to deface the runes on the wall, turn to section 117.

107

Its touch is cold. At first the shadows keep their distance. Then one simply flows through the mace and touches Alynn. Something is pulled from inside the cleric with a sickly wrenching tear. He fights down a wave of nausea.

Spinning, he swings at the shadow behind him, only to feel the other's frigid touch. His mace grows very heavy. Each swing becomes slower and more difficult than the last.

The next touch doesn't feel as painfully cold; but is almost like a caress. Alynn dimly realizes his body feels distant and weak. He is too tired to care. His world narrows to a badly lit corridor with a ragged black silhouette dancing in its center.

The world contracts again, and Alynn welcomes the dive into the darkness. For a moment he feels nothing. Then he slides easily to where there are no more moments.

Turn to section 29.

108

Alynn realizes he is too far away. The spell will be completed before he can get close enough to stop it.

Section 108

If the last spell is anything to judge by, this one is likely to be deadly. Already, the air ahead of the running cleric shimmers with the faint image of whirling blades. As he hurries forward, the insubstantial blades pass through him unfelt. With each step the blades become clearer and more solid. Long before he is beyond them, the blades will have materialized.

There is no warning of the lightning bolt. Concerned with the rapidly materializing barrier of blades, Alynn is aware of the lightning only after it has struck. The bolt strikes his opponent with such force it throws the older man against the wall. The body slides slowly into a heap on the floor next to the open Demon Gate. The force of the blast slams Alynn to a stop.

There is no question the other man is dead. The evil one's body has been nearly torn apart by the force of the blast. Part of his chest and one arm have been completely vaporized. The area around the wound is scorched and still smoldering. A jagged line has been etched on the stone behind where the bolt burst through his body and spent itself on the granite wall.

Ready to face this new and more powerful menace, Alynn turns, mace raised. He thinks in passing that his metal chain mail will be poor protection against a demon capable of throwing lightning bolts. Still there is no time to discard it. He completes the turn expecting to face at least a lesser demon.

To Alynn's amazement, all he sees is Lyla, calmly entering the room through the doorway. Either she did not see the lightning bolt or she is not concerned about it. She does not even seem afraid, but her step is slow and her shoulders sag. The dark-haired Gama meets the cleric's look, her eyes full of sadness and concern.

"You?" the cleric asks, his voice breaking. Could Lyla have been the source of the bolt?

The woman says nothing, merely smiles weakly.

"Did you do that?" Alynn asks, recovering some control over his voice. His eyes drift to the sprawling form of his antagonist. "The Darklord...?"

"That wasn't him."

"Who, then?"

"Trancelius, the cleric of some disgusting and obscure cult."

Section 108

Alynn continues to look from the body to Lyla and back again.

"He has been a minion of the Darklord for decades, though he was mostly out for himself," she explains, almost apologizing. "The world is better off without his sort. I hope his own god has him now." The last words sound more like a curse than a comment. Then her anger fades to be replaced again by a look of distress.

By this time the darkly clad woman is standing at Alynn's side. As she starts toward the glowing Demon Gate, he follows.

"How did you...?" he begins to ask again.

"We had better get that Ankh out of the center of the Gate and get it closed," she interrupts. "You heard what he was summoning."

The green lines shimmer and dance in front of them as they get closer. The bars of light give the impression of great power, yet they are made of such a pure radiance that the area behind them is visible through them. The humans' hair stands and dances from their proximity to the forces unleashed here. Beyond the Gate Alynn can see shapes that resemble pastel clouds. They twist and swirl in a hypnotic pattern. In a few more steps the cleric and his companion are standing in front of the Gate.

"The only way to end this forever is to destroy that Ankh," Lyla observes. "The Gate and Ankh must never be joined again."

After all his efforts to obtain the Ankh, Alynn is reluctant to touch the looped cross suspended in the gateway. But as he looks at it, the cleric begins to understand that he must destroy this beautifully crafted symbol of the god he worships. To do so seems like a sacrilege.

"I hope Cearn will forgive me," he mumbles to himself.

Cautiously the man bends forward, intending to pull the Ankh from the Demon Gate. The green bars of light emanate from the Ankh's five points. He tries to grab it below the crossbars and so avoid having to touch the grid. Remembering who was being summoned, and

Section 108

might appear at any time, Alynn is reluctant to step closer to the Demon Gate. Instead, the cleric leans forward until he is almost off balance. His fingers are scant inches from the Ankh when he feels hands shove him forward.

Overbalancing, he stumbles toward the glowing Demon Gate. The Ankh falls past still a few inches too far to reach as the unexpected push sends him tumbling through the glowing bars and into the plane where demons dwell.

Fear washes over Alynn like a wave of cold water. Trying to turn, the cleric finds himself floating as if suspended in a sea of air. No matter how he thrashes, he cannot move against the unresisting air around him. The hairs on his neck rise. He is sure a messenger of death waits just out of sight behind him. Twisting his neck to a painful angle, Alynn looks around frantically, expecting to see his personal nightmare, the ten-tongued demon, Phameet, looming overhead. To his relief, he is alone. His surge of relief turns to dismay as he surveys his surroundings.

There seems to be no ground or solid matter of any sort, just formless wisps of cloud weaving through one another. Each wisp is a slightly different shade of green. Over his shoulder the cleric can see the outline of the Demon Gate. The Ankh at its center appears to be the only solid object in this universe. Struggle as he may, the cleric is unable even to turn. Then he hears Lyla's voice. She sounds only inches away.

"I'm sorry, Alynn." The dark-haired woman's voice is filled with emotion. "I don't know if you can hear this, but I had no choice but to betray you. No choice. The Ankh has powers you can never guess at. We need those powers. Blium says we have no choice, and he is our leader.

"I should have killed you, but I was too weak." There is a long pause. "I don't know if I could have succeeded. You're so damned righteous and determined that nothing stopped you. You never would have given me the Ankh. You left me no choice." There is another long pause.

"Well"—the Gama woman speaks between sobs

Section 108

now—"I...must...I have...a duty....Maybe...someday...in another life."

Lyla's hands appear and wrap themselves around the bottom of the double Ankh. They tense as if pulling against a great weight, and then the Gate vanishes.

Alynn finds himself floating among the ever changing almost-clouds. He has no way to determine if he is moving or if they are.

For a time he lets grief blind him. He has lost, and worse yet, lived to know it. Lyla will become a bitter memory made worse by deep feelings for her that have been growing in him. Curled up into a ball, he lets the colored wisps flow past him unobserved. Being nowhere and doing nothing fits his mood. He lets himself mourn.

He rises from his state of apathy suddenly when a distant form rushes past, but he cannot be sure of its shape. Chillingly he remembers a Demonlord was being summoned from this place. Somewhere on this plane Phameet, the deceiver of men, lives in his tower of lies. Alynn may be drifting toward the accursed one without knowing it.

Taking a renewed interest in surviving, Alynn begins to look about. The clouds take on a red tint, then purple, but he has no idea what this might mean. If he is to die in this place, he resolves to make Phameet pay. Trying to look determined, the cleric hefts his mace and looks around him warily.

"Well, I told you so." Rhea's voice is loud and mocking, but stronger now than it was at the Lesser Abbey. He straightens in shock and then relaxes, smiling.

"Rhea!" The cleric's tone reflects his relief. "I thought all was lost."

"Very nearly so," the voice sounds stern and a bit disappointed. "I tried to warn you about that woman. You mortals seem to lose all perspective. Do you find a pretty face and body that hard to resist?"

Alynn doesn't reply. In view of his present situation, any protest will sound a bit hollow. The silence stretches on for an uncomfortably long time. He knows now why Rhea's voice sounded so loud. This plane is totally silent. All the little sounds that everyone take for granted

Section 108

are missing. There are no insects or leaves here. There is not even the gentle rush of a breeze. Not even the beating of his heart breaks the silence. While searching vainly for a pulse, Alynn realizes he is not breathing. After a nervous wait, he accepts that here he doesn't need to. The cleric slaps the head of his mace against his palm and is rewarded with a faint but reassuring sound. Then there is only waiting and hoping he has not been abandoned. Finally Rhea breaks the silence.

"No more time for you to drift aimlessly. You have to get moving," she admonishes.

"I'd love to," Alynn replies, waving his arms and legs to demonstrate his difficulty.

"This isn't your limited material plane," Rhea explains. "Here thought rules, with other things you have no words for. All you have to do is will yourself forward. I will be out of reach again for a short time."

"I can breathe here," Alynn tells himself. He takes an experimental breath, and nothing seems different. The air smells of cinnamon with a hint of the sea. "But I don't need to," he tells himself, and he can feel his chest stop pumping. Time passes and the man feels no different.

The cleric concentrates on moving, and to his amazement begins to drift slowly forward. He closes his eyes and paints for himself the picture of him soaring gracefully through the multicolored sky. After the grim reality of the last three days, everything takes on a pleasant dreamlike quality. The thrill of effortless flying nearly makes the man forget his wounds and the urgency of the mission he has not yet completed.

"This is fun!" Alynn exclaims while willing a banking weave to the left and down. By now he is moving through the clouds at a respectable rate.

The clouds take on a bluish tint, and Alynn slowly becomes aware they are no longer drifting randomly. All the wisps are converging to his left. He wills himself into a wide turn. Seconds later he sees the hole.

There is no other way to describe it. Ahead of him is a jagged tear in the cloud-filled sky. The swirling masses of the almost-clouds are disappearing into the hole. As they rush toward it, they form a whirlpool of

Section 108

pastels. For the first time Alynn can feel a breeze, a sensation of movement as a gentle pull tugs him toward the gap. Curious, he lets himself drift closer to the phenomenon.

"Get away from there!" Rhea's voice is harsh and urgent.

Concentrating, the cleric wills himself to stop. He spins until he is facing away from the opening and pictures himself dashing away to calmer skies. Opening his eyes, the cleric looks back over his shoulder. To Alynn's horror, he sees that his movement toward the black gap has not slowed. If anything, he is being sucked in even more quickly. The feeling now is one of falling uncontrollably into the distant maelstrom.

"Rhea!" he yells. His voice seems lost in the formlessness. The rent in the sky is closer now. The clouds around Alynn have darkened until they appear almost solid. He can distinctly feel the firm pull of the hole on his robe and hair; his mace trails back toward it, dragging his arm behind him.

Once again he glances over his shoulder. Now he can see inside the opening. The clouds seem to fade and then dissolve as they pass into it, leaving inside a velvety darkness broken by a lone orange spot. The hole now fills a quarter of the sky behind him as the cleric renews his efforts to escape.

"You have drifted too close," Rhea instructs calmly. "There is only one chance for you to break free. You will have to use the pull of the well to throw yourself past it. It's dangerous and will take every bit of your concentration and courage."

"What is that thing?" Alynn demands, his voice breaking in near panic. "If I'm going to die inside it, I'd at least like to know what it is!"

"Did you ever wonder where universes come from?" Rhea replies in a casual, almost lecturing manner. "This plane is where the something comes from that appears from nothing when a universe is formed. That is a cosmic well.

"Inside that gap is a cosmic egg almost ready to burst. Like all young things it is very hungry. It wants to gather all the ether it can to create the biggest and

Section 108

most varied universe possible."

Alynn is close enough now to see that the orange dot has taken on an oval shape. Waves of less solid blackness appear to be descending on a bright orange egg in its center. The egg ripples and grows perceptibly larger as each new wave strikes it.

"Is that thing alive?" Alynn asks, so enthralled he momentarily forgets his own danger.

"Of course, and most aware."

"You said it's going to burst and form an entire universe?"

"Of course, how did you think they start?"

Alynn has to admit he's really never wondered. Universes always seemed beyond his concern. Instead of replying he watches, fascinated.

"Isn't it aware it will die when it bursts?" he finally asks, still staring at the glowing egg.

"Why would it do that?" Rhea sounds genuinely surprised. Then she laughs. "Oh, the explosion. Where do you think gods come from? They can't all be around from the start. Why, this plane would be crowded with deities waiting for their universes."

Neither speaks for a second. The cleric tries to accept the fact he is watching the birth of a god.

"Am I dead? Is this a dream?" he asks in awed tones.

"Hardly, but it's time for you to do something or you will be. If you don't start now, you'll soon find out more about the process than you will like." Rhea warns.

"Would I be aware of the whole universe, part of the god?" Alynn asks, nearly mesmerized by the grandeur of the concept.

"Your awareness will be spread thinly throughout every atom of the creation. Sometimes I suspect a particularly stubborn being drifted into the egg that formed the human plane...A very stubborn one.

"Now listen carefully.

"You are being pulled toward the nexus at an ever increasing rate. Already it is too strong for your will to overcome, and I cannot help you. Stop fighting and let it pull you. Instead, use all your concentration to angle toward the right side.

"You want to just miss the rim and be thrown past.

Section 108

You should end up somewhere close to where you need to be. The Demon Gate is still open and time is running out.

"Be very careful. Even the edges of the well can absorb anything that touches them."

Only with an effort does the man takes his eyes off the cosmic egg. Looking around, he is frightened to see the hole now fills half the sky ahead. Willing himself to face right, Alynn concentrates on the image of moving toward the right side of the opening.

There are sounds now. The sounds of tension building, the groans and creaks of twisted space. Without asking, Alynn knows the noises are audible through the overlap of this and the universe about to be formed.

He risks a glance at the egg. It is pulsing now. The egg shudders with each expansion. On impulse the cleric pulls a small double ankh from his pocket. It is a smaller version of the holy symbol he uses when invoking the Turn Undead spell. Each symbol represents and may even, he guesses, contain a tiny bit of Cearn. He is sworn to spread the worship of Cearn everywhere. Why not to a new universe? He tosses the tiny ankh toward the egg. It diminishes rapidly and then is lost.

"I'm not sure that was a good idea," Rhea comments. "But no doubt the results will be interesting."

Alynn has no time to comment as the gaping hole and its jagged edge are drawing close. The blackness fills the sky, and ether pours past him with a thundering roar.

The cleric tries to focus every bit of his awareness on moving across the opening and past the side. He repeats and repeats again images of himself almost, but not quite, touching the edge of the pulsing darkness and sailing on to safety.

Roll 3 D6

If the total is the same as or less than Alynn's value for Intelligence, turn to section 123.

If the total is greater than Alynn's Intelligence value, turn to section 125.

Section 109

109

It is hard to see the spiders in the half-light. The web dances as they rush toward him. Bracing himself, the cleric watches the eight-legged monsters as they dance gracefully down their webs toward him. Their black carapaces glisten above hairy legs that seem almost impossibly thin for the bulk of their wide bodies. When they are almost close enough to strike, he steps to one side.

He is unaware of the third spider until he feels the weight of it landing on his shoulder. Instinctively, he throws himself against the cavern wall in an effort to crush the monster clinging to his shoulder and back. Lyla's warning scream echoes almost deafeningly.

To support so large a boneless body, the shell of the spider is very strong. Even the full force of the impact against the wall fails to smash the arachnid. Alynn is trying to scrape the battered monster off against the wall when it finds a gap in his battered chain mail.

The sting as its mandibles tear at his shoulder hurts badly, but this seems like nothing compared to the agony he feels seconds later when the spider injects its poison into his body. Each heartbeat seems to last a pain-filled minute as the poison is carried through his bloodstream to every part of his body. With each beat of his heart the torture spreads.

Nausea rises, and Alynn tastes the bitter rush of bile as his stomach empties. The muscles of his back twitch spasmodically until they lock in a cramped knot. The mace clatters to the floor. He feels the other spiders climbing up one leg, but his eyes seem able to focus only on the stone wall ahead. He tries to swing his mace, but his arm will not respond, and he has no will left to demand its obedience. Somewhere far away a man's voice screams. Absently, beyond his own pain, Alynn wonders at the intensity of the torture the screaming man must be suffering. His innate sympathy moves him to wish the sufferer an end to such agony. The scream ends with a rattle, and he gets his wish.

Turn to section 29.

Section 110, 111

110

"Down," Alynn yells, pushing Lyla forward. The dark-haired woman screams as she stumbles to the floor near the coins. The hum of the crossbow bolt whistling past them is punctuated by a loud crack as it smashes into the wall a few inches behind the crouching cleric. Dust and shards of rock splatter over him.

"Oh," Lyla says, staring at the small crater on the wall and the mangled bolt on the floor by Alynn's feet.

Turn to section 91.

111

Slowly, carefully, and silently, the ancient door opens. The back of a blue-clad man is visible in the large room beyond. It seems a very long time, with each second threatening discovery, before Alynn can step through.

The walls are panels of granite; the floor is composed of seamless, smooth black stone. Four columns support a ceiling of the same smooth stone as the floor. The far wall and the kneeling figure are more than fifty feet away. The chanter's reflection extends yards toward Alynn and Lyla on the highly polished floor. As they watch, the entire room fills with an unnatural greenish light. This emanates from the runes inscribed on the wall in front of the man.

The Gate has been activated.

Beyond the bars of green light, swirling clouds are visible. Alynn and Lyla watch in horror, expecting a grotesque demon to appear at any second. The figure on the floor begins a different and more guttural chant. One word is repeated, the name Phameet, one of the most powerful Demon Princes, a creature whose spider-demons once often haunted his nightmares.

Knowing the demon might answer the summons at any moment, Alynn abandons stealth and rushes toward the bent figure.

The blue-clad man spins, still kneeling. His eyes go wide with surprise. He half rises, and the men lock

Section 112

eyes. A small smile appears on the older man's face. Breaking eye contact, he begins gesturing. His hands move with a practiced skill the other knows he cannot match. The gestures end with a dramatic uplifting of the older man's left arm. The air above Alynn's head begins to crackle.

"Watch out!" Lyla shrieks.

Roll 3 D6.

If the total is the same or less than Alynn's value for Dexterity, turn to section 115.

If the total is greater than Alynn's Dexterity value, turn to section 104.

112

As the light flickers out, Alynn pushes open the left-hand door. The room beyond appears empty. Tall windows set high in the wall allow in faint starlight. In the center of the room is a jagged hole in the floor. Around the hole are piles of rock and dirt.

Stepping through the door, Alynn tenses. At first he feels nothing.

"You're glowing," Lyla blurts out.

The cleric is surrounded by a red glow. It outlines his body from head to foot. Even as he watches, the glow grows brighter. More confused than frightened, he stands and watches. The glow becomes bright enough for him to see each thread of his robe. Looking down, Alynn notices drops of sweat on his arms.

He is growing rapidly warmer. As the glow grows bright enough to cast faint shadows on the wall, the heat becomes painful. A few seconds later the cleric feels as if he is being submerged in boiling water. Still the light and heat grow. The light is now a bright yellow, almost white. Lyla has to squint to look at the suffering cleric.

Swaying, nearly unconscious, the priest sees the frayed threads of his robe begin to smolder. Brushing the sweat from his forehead he can feel heat radiating from his hair. Leaning against the stone wall, the cleric sinks to his knees. The world is filled with nothing but

Section 113, 114, 115

the heat. He can feel the skin on every part of his body blistering. The light is so bright he cannot open his eyes.

Finally the man sags and falls unconscious. For only a few seconds more the intense light fills the chamber. Then it fades rapidly. Entering through the right door, Lyla hurries to the fallen cleric. His hair is singed, and tiny blisters cover his face. Concerned, the woman touches Alynn's forehead. Drawing her dagger she settles down beside him.

Alynn has taken 2 D6 of damage. Roll 2 D6 dice and subtract the total from the cleric's hit points. If Alynn has been killed by the trap, turn to section 29.

If Alynn survives, turn to section 137.

113

Roll 3 D6.

If the total is the same as or less than Alynn's value for Intelligence, turn to section 86.

If the total is greater than Alynn's Intelligence value, turn to section 97.

114

SKELETON
To Hit Alynn: 13   To Be Hit: 10   Hit Points: 3
Damage with Swords: 1 D6

Like most undead, these skeletons will fight until destroyed. Both may attack each round.

If Alynn defeats the skeletons, turn to section 46.

If Alynn is killed, turn to section 29.

115

Diving to the side, Alynn doesn't see the sparks over his head coalesce into a floor-to-ceiling rod. Before his eyes can focus on the radiant green pole, it bursts apart sending sparks in all directions. Each spark ignites the

Section 116

air around it. Looking back, Alynn can see a ten-foot pillar of raging fire. The waves of heat and the nearly deafening roar send him scuttling along the floor.

Over the noise from the pillar Alynn can hear the old man laughing. Such a pillar is a product of clerical magic, the priest of Cearn realizes. It seems terrible to him that the Darklord might be a priest like himself. Anger rises, and the roar of blood in Alynn's ears drowns out even the rumble from the pillar of fire. Here is a man, not a beast; a man can be made to bleed and pay for what he did to the Lesser Abbey.

Hefting his mace, the younger cleric pulls himself to his feet. Crouching, ready to dodge or attack, he moves toward the laughing man. That silences the laughter, but the amused look never leaves the older man's eyes as he stands before the Gate and begins another series of unfamiliar gestures. The sound of the pillar of fire fades as the man concentrates on conjuring the new spell.

Turn to section 108.

116

The dust is still settling behind him when Alynn turns down the road to Terverni. He wonders if anyone will ever believe what he has done. Perhaps Orlow might understand, but as a lowly priest of Cearn, Alynn thinks it unlikely that he will get an audience with the great Wizard.

"You're not so lowly," a familiar voice corrects.

"Rhea!"

"You have done far more than any other man would have been able to." The woman's voice is filled with praise. "Never has a follower of Cearn done so much to protect his fellow man. Does it really matter if the others are aware of it? Cearn is."

"What makes you so sure?" the weary cleric asks pointedly. The danger is over, and he no longer fears losing Rhea's assistance. He still knows virtually nothing about her—except that she claims to know what his god feels.

"I suppose you have earned an answer," she says,

Section 116

"though it will be a long time before wise men understand what happened here."

"Who are you, or rather what are you?" the cleric demands. So much of what Rhea is saying makes no sense.

"I am one manifestation of Cearn, your god."

"But you are a woman," Alynn answers, confused. "Cearn is a man."

"Foolish human. Do you really think the gods are male or female? We are gods. Only you humans try to attach a gender to us. I am neither a man nor a woman, or more accurately, I am both. It is more important to ask if a god is at all, than to ask what he is."

"Then why do you have a woman's voice?" the man questions, still unsure if he can believe what Rhea is telling him.

"I used a woman's voice because in an abbey filled with men, you would notice it. There was no time to announce myself, nor could you afford to hesitate." Her voice becomes deep and totally masculine. "If you had not reacted instantly to my first warning, I would have needed a new champion, and you would have joined those others who died in the Lesser Abbey."

"Why couldn't you save them, too?" he asks, fighting down bitterness. "My friends, my world, they all died and you did nothing. Couldn't you have performed a miracle?"

"There is a cost, a price both gods and men must pay for their free will. The massacre at the abbey was part of that cost. I wish I could have done more. I could not.

"Also the Ankh, while the Gate was still intact, kept me from doing more than I did."

"But that Gate opened onto the plane of demons," Alynn protests. "Why would it affect you? You say you are a god, but a demon?"

"There is less difference between the two than you might think. The gods of any era are nearly always doomed to be the demons of the next. If a god is neither he nor she, why must we be either all good or completely evil? Why do you humans always try to explain the unexplainable in terms of yourselves? Perhaps in that other universe, the one you so impetuously inter-

Section 117

jected a bit of me into, things will be different." The voice becomes once more that of Rhea. It speaks softly and with perceptible sympathy.

"The Demon Gate is closed and will not be opened again. You should not have won, but you did, and because of this I can take a more active role in your world again.

"If there is a true value to you humans, it may be that you never admit defeat. You have won this time and earned your rest.

For a few seconds Alynn wonders if he should protest. He is a long day's walk on the wrong side of the Mistwall, and the Darklord is likely to desire his revenge.

"You are safe now," Rhea reassures the tired cleric. "Trust me this one more time."

Having just entered the area where green grass once again grows, Alynn settles down on the first patch he crosses. It is painful to pull the remnants of his chain mail off his lacerated skin, but when it clanks to the ground, he feels as if a burden has been lifted from him. It is all right, he decides, to simply lie down and sleep. The world is once more safe, he remembers proudly, because of his efforts.

The cleric's eyes drift shut, and he doesn't see the dome of soft yellow light form protectively over him. Nor does he notice that same light gently pass over his wounds, healing and then restoring his battered and torn muscles.

It may be just as well that the exhausted cleric also fails to hear Rhea's next comment.

"Rest and heal, my Hero, for there is one thing the gods do share with men, the gift of laughter. This time we tweaked the nose of Darkness.

"Wait until next time."

The END

117

The stone wall proves to be as solid as it appears. Each smashing blow chips away only a few of the intricate runes. Every few minutes Alynn stops and looks around for the minion of the Darklord that Rhea warned

Section 118, 119

him about.

After much hard labor, Alynn succeeds in defacing that part of the pattern where the Ankh once rested. He almost doesn't hear the scrape of the demon's hoof over the harsh sound his own breath. Spinning, he finds himself looking at the long, daggerlike claws of the vulture-demon. The creature is standing only a step away. Instinctively the cleric swings his mace, and it glances off the monster's head.

VULTURE-DEMON
To Hit Alynn: 10   To Be Hit: 14   Hit Points: 11
Damage from Claws: 1 D6; from Teeth: 1 D6

The vulture-demon will attack twice each round, once with claws and once with teeth. It has been sent to kill whomever if finds near the Demon Gate and then to recover the Ankh. It cannot return to its own plane until the Ankh is returned. It will fight until destroyed.

If Alynn defeats the vulture-demon, turn to section 132.

If Alynn is killed, turn to section 29.

118

It takes a total of 50 hit points of damage for Alynn to completely deface the runes on the wall. Roll 1 D6 for each time Alynn attacks the wall. After each five attacks, turn to section 132.

If Alynn succeeds in smashing all of the runes on the wall, turn to section 119.

119

The cleric looks at the wall with satisfaction. That panel will not be used as a Demon Gate for a very long time. At that moment, the glittering form of yet another materializing vulture-demon makes him hurry from the chamber. He is climbing into the abbey when he hears the enraged cry of the monster. Battered as he is, Alynn doubles his speed, rushes through the temple, and bursts out of the abbey.

Section 120

The cleric doesn't stop running until he reaches the graveyard wall. The low rumble begins slowly. As the sound builds, the cleric finds he has trouble standing. Clinging to the wall for balance, Alynn watches as the temple walls cave in and its roof collapses with a loud roar. A section of the wall to the left of the abbey's entrance disintegrates into a chest-high pile of rubble.

The priest cannot help but smile. It appears, he tells himself, that the Darklord is frustrated. It is long minutes before the ground is once more peaceful. There is no sign of the demon. Alynn hopes it perished in the tunnels below.

Turn to section 116.

120

The vulture-demon is only half materialized when the cleric swings his mace at it. Sparks dance, and the mace thuds solidly against the demon's skull. A birdlike cry of rage fills the room. The form of the demon is clearer now. The demon is much taller than the human, though more slightly built. Its thin neck seems hardly capable of supporting so massive a head. The head itself is dominated by tiny eyes and a grotesque tooth-filled beak. The demon's hands end in long, daggerlike claws. Blood from the wound on its head drips pale green on the glossy black floor.

The half-formed demon stumbles forward under the blow, and Alynn's second swing passes harmlessly above it. Hurrying to maintain his advantage, the cleric follows and brings his mace down on the back of the demon's beaked head. He hears the bones of its neck crunch. Backing away, the cleric expects the demon to fall.

Instead, the monster rears up to its full height and roars. It steps toward the cleric, and for a few seconds Alynn can only dodge a flurry of frantic attacks. Then, just as unexpectedly, it topples over. Moments later it is dissolving into a yellow dust, which then vanishes.

For several minutes the battered cleric can only stand and pant. Then the air once again begins to shimmer.

Section 121, 122

Quickly he pulls the scroll from his pocket and begins to read.

Turn to section 134.

121

The demonic spider closes the gap between them with little effort. Cautiously Alynn wills himself upward, above the range of its spiny legs. The larger monster does not turn to follow, but reaches up with its taloned hands. A cloud of red begins to pour from its nostrils. Alynn fears poison gas until he remembers he is not breathing.

Then the demon hovers a few feet below him, and there is no more time to use magic. He swings the mace, but it passes through the spider body with no apparent effect. The demon's clawed hand tears a jagged line across the cleric's extended arm. Then Alynn hears Rhea speak.

"Think about the mace hitting the demon. This is a place where the thought is as important as the action," Rhea advises. The cleric's second blow lands with a satisfying impact on the demon's scaly chest.

SPIDER-DEMON
To Hit Alynn: 10   To Be Hit: 11   Hit Points: 12
Damage per Round: 1 D6

The demon has the first attack.

If Alynn defeats the demon, turn to section 124.

If Alynn is killed, turn to section 29.

122

It is dawn when Alynn leaves the abbey. He has no idea where Lyla has gone. The best course, he decides, is to go to Terverni and tell Orlow what has occurred. Tired and badly wounded, he can only walk a few miles a day.

Without a guide, Alynn wanders for three days in the Mistwall. In his nightmares the twisting mists become the ethereal clouds, and the spider-demon has

Section 123

returned for revenge. Too many times he awakens with no recollection of having fallen. When he finally crosses into Terverni it seems likely it is too late. The moon was full when he first entered the ancient abbey; now it is dark and new.

The cleric hears a deep roar. At first he thinks it is thunder, but there are no clouds. Then he wonders if the rumble is part of some magical battle. Finally the cleric sees an immense form towering above him.

The demon Phameet stands taller than a hundred men when manifested on the material plane. A touch from any of its eight massive legs dissolves all living flesh. Phameet seems unaware of Alynn as it steps on the cowering cleric. Uncaring destruction is the mark of the Princes of Chaos. Then again, the Demonlord might have been taking revenge for its slain lesser demon. It matters little to Alynn as his part in this cycle of life ends in a burst of searing agony. Phameet strides toward Terverni. A horde of lesser demons skitter and crawl in its wake.

Turn to section 29.

123

The throbbing blackness rushes at the cleric. Bits of cloud rush past him too quickly to register. Sweat appears on Alynn's forehead as he concentrates on safely crossing the immense gap.

The image inside his head becomes clear. The weight of his body slips away, feeling like a gentle caress. The ethereal roar diminishes to a distant background murmur. Alynn sees himself as a mote drifting quickly across the immense and growing opening. He wills himself to move faster, and the mote nearly doubles its speed. Feeling cause for hope, the cleric studies his surroundings.

From his new perspective the primal well resembles a jagged eye, its pulsing orange cornea seems to be watching the tiny floating speck that is Alynn. Close to the edge, he is confident he will pass by without harm.

Section 124

"Don't you ever blink?" he asks the eye playfully. "You could at least wish me luck." He feels a bit silly talking to a miles-wide eye that is really the god of a universe that doesn't exist yet.

"I hope your universe turns out well," he wishes sincerely.

To the cleric's amazement the orange egg seems to pause for a short instant in its quest for matter. A tiny orange and yellow comet bursts from the glowing shape and speeds toward the tiny mote of his body.

He tenses, almost losing his concentration when it hits, but all he feels is a gentle tug. Looking down at himself, Alynn sees his body is surrounded by a gentle nimbus of orange light. Like a glowing speck he is moving even more rapidly toward the edge and safety.

"I've never heard of a god performing a miracle before it even existed," Rhea comments. There seems to be a new respect in her voice. "I hope you can live up to the honor."

Alynn resists the urge to observe that he hopes he lives at all.

Turn to section 136.

124

The spider-demon surges forward in an attempt to use its greater size to overwhelm the man. On the material plane where both would be limited to moving in three dimensions, this strategy would likely have worked. Alynn realizes this demon is used to battling humans in his world. Here, where he can dodge and flit about, the monster's size gives it little advantage. If anything, the cleric finds he is able to maneuver a bit more quickly than his demonic opponent.

Alynn earns a bloody gouge below his ribs when he tries to stand up and trade blows with the stronger monster. Dodging away, he decides always to end up slightly above its reptilian head. Because the human is forced to avoid the demon's claws, the battle settles down to a series of rushes by the demon and soaring evasions by the cleric.

Finally the demon, perhaps through frustration,

Section 124

rushes past and below the evading cleric. The man finds himself hovering over its unprotected back. Neither its reptilian arms nor its spider legs can reach above and behind itself. Mace ready, Alynn dives toward the chitinous covering.

The mace strikes with the full force of the cleric's swooping body behind it. The handle stings. Had it not been secured by its strap, the mace could have been lost. The demon's smooth shell bursts, and the spider legs twitch and curl. Before the demon can spin over, the cleric is far above it. The joy of battle has left the demon's eyes. Now rage and cunning dominate its expression.

For minutes they weave through the pastel clouds, the man striving to gain the advantage, the demon to face his faster and more agile opponent. Twice Alynn is nearly caught in the creature's clawed hands. Finally he feints with his mace and sails over its head to strike it where the reptilian back joins the spider shell. Its spine cracks, and the creature begins to drift, its many arms and legs dangling loosely.

The cleric waits for the demon to fall and then realizes the absurdity of his action. Drifting himself, he should know there is no place on this plane for the demon to fall to, nor is there any gravity to pull it down—whatever direction down might be.

"Rhea, I won!" he boasts. "I won!"

"Congratulations," the woman's voice answers. "Now you must hurry. I have found a way for you to return to the abbey. A way you can bring your body through also."

"There will be no pain?" he asks cautiously.

"No pain, though there will be danger," she warns.

"What now?" The cleric feels almost confident as he drifts above the slain demon. "Another of these spider-demons?"

"Possibly, or worse," Rhea answers deflatingly. "The Darklord is aware his plan failed. By now he knows someone has thwarted his scheme. He will know this means Trancelius is dead. He will send something even more powerful to investigate."

"How do I get back?" Alynn asks, not wanting to

Section 124

dwell on what might await him there.

"There is a sort of gate formed by the forces powering the traps in some doors. These forces tap the energy of this plane. With my help you can slip through the opening and return to your earth. There is some danger, but less than staying here. This spider-demon is one of the less powerful residents of this place. Phameet will discover soon that it is missing and send others to investigate."

"How many more are there like this one?" the man inquires, looking nervously at the large body. The thrill of his victory has faded, and only the pain of his wounds remains.

"Several million of that type of demon," Rhea answers casually. "It really is one of the less common types nowadays. Most of the really fierce ones hunt them for pleasure."

"I think its time to try that gate," Alynn decides quickly. "Let's get going."

When he reaches the gap, Alynn is hardly surprised to see another hole in the fabric of this universe. He is beginning to form an image of this plane as a very large and colorful blanket full of moth holes. He hopes Rhea isn't too insulted at the concept.

Through this gap he can see the room where the tunnel enters the abbey. The room appears empty, though only part of it is visible.

The opening itself is oval and just large enough to slip through. He touches the edge with the handle of his mace and the mace pulls back half an inch shorter.

"You sure I'll fit?" Alynn asks.

Rhea ignores the question. Instead she urges him to hurry, pointing out how vital it is he reach the gate before the Darklord sends another demon.

"Every time you fail to heed my advice, you suffer for it. Now hurry. I have already explained the fate that awaits your country if the Demon Gate is ever fully opened."

"But what can I do?" the cleric protests. "Lyla has the Ankh. She could be halfway to Malri by now."

"There is a way. You have to find it."

"Can't you just tell me?"

Section 125

"No."

"Why not?"

"I also can't tell you why not. It has something to do with your being able to make your own decisions."

"As though I've had a choice." The cleric tries not to sound bitter, but his wounds hurt and he is very tired. Still he wills himself into the opening, cautious to avoid the edges.

"Be careful," Rhea admonishes him. "I won't be able to talk to you very often once you pass through."

By now the cleric's feet are entering the oval portal.

"One more thing," she adds. "When you get halfway through, the laws of your plane will take over. Try not to touch the edge of the portal when you fall."

The first pull of the promised weight stops Alynn's reply. If Rhea is reading his mind, he decides, it is probably just as well she can't talk to him anymore. Then he concentrates on being ready for the return of his normal weight.

He twists within the narrow tube, trying to avoid its edges as he falls through. Things happens so quickly that he has no time to be careful. One moment he is still among lavender clouds; the next he is in the center of a long tunnel.

Roll 3 D6.

If the total is the same as or less than Alynn's value for Dexterity, turn to section 106.

If the total is greater than Alynn's Dexterity value, turn to section 135.

125

The hungry blackness rushes at the cleric. Bits of cloud streak past too quickly to register. Sweat appears on Alynn's forehead as he concentrates on safely crossing the immense gap.

The roar and the speeding clouds distract him, so Alynn closes his eyes in an effort to concentrate entirely on willing his passage. He never sees the edge as it throbs outward just as he sails past it.

Section 126, 127

Only his thigh and hip brush against the jagged darkness that forms the side of the opening. Blue-white light flares from where they touch. The heat generated by the half-inch of flesh and muscle dissolving into primal matter cauterizes the wound even as it is formed. The cleric's scream of pain is lost in the ether's deafening roar.

Alynn will receive 1 D6 of damage from brushing the edge.

If Alynn survives the mishap, turn to section 136.

If Alynn is killed, turn to section 29.

126

The figure reaches down toward the stricken cleric. Before it touches him, Allyn collapses onto the floor. His body twitches spasmodically, throwing sparks from the smoldering cloth on his back. Then he lies unmoving.

The glowing form hesitates for a second, almost as if studying what remains of the cleric. Then it straightens and faces the blue-clad figure by the Gate. It raises a hand and gestures as if to cast a spell of its own. Then, as if disturbed, it stops conjuring and glances upward. The radiant creature's shoulders sag, and it fades. Within seconds, the blackened body of the cleric is alone where it fell.

Turn to section 29.

127

Hurriedly the cleric wills himself backward. The demon's eyes fill with joy when it sees its victim flee. While it closes in, Alynn casts a Sanctuary spell. He finishes with the standard invocation of Cearn's protection and an extra prayer that the god might help him.

For a nervous moment the cleric wonders if the spell will work in this strange place with its new laws. Then he feels the relaxed peacefulness the Sanctuary spell always gives him. He looks down and sees that his

Section 128

body is surrounded by a nimbus of yellow light.

The demon stops and pokes carefully at the glowing figure floating ahead of him. The chitinous legs stop at the edge of the light. In the next minutes the demon circles the man, prodding and searching for any opening in his defense. Each time it fails, Alynn's morale rises. He finds it almost amusing to watch the gigantic demon scuttling about in frustration. He cannot hide the smile this thought brings.

The smile fades when the demon settles himself a few yards in front of Alynn and begins to wait. It apparently knows that Sanctuary spells last for a limited time.

The look in the creature's eyes is most unpleasant as the two drift through an ever changing backdrop of pastel clouds. Finally the light from the spell begins to fade.

If Alynn should cast his Spirit Hammer spell, turn to section 25.

If Alynn should cast a Turn Undead spell, turn to section 129.

If Alynn should close in and fight the demon, turn to section 121.

128

The cleric tries to remember if Rhea said anything about how to end the threat of the Demon Gate. He recalls her initial warnings and the fall of the abbey. The warnings about Lyla and their many conversations while he floated through the ethereal plane seem to offer no clue. Then he recalls the instructions to take the scroll from the mummy. He might still have it. With nervous hands he searches his belt and finds the silver scroll case.

If Alynn has not yet used the scroll, turn to section 133.

If Alynn has already used the scroll, turn to section 131.

Section 129

129

"Cearn, I hope you are listening," Alynn mumbles to the swirling clouds. Then he begins the chant for the Turn Undead spell. The demon towers over the smaller human. It is hard to read any expression on the scarred features, but there is no mistaking the happiness in its eyes. This creature is attacking for the sheer joy of it. How appropriate for a demon of chaos, Alynn tells himself, hardly comforted by the thought.

When the chant ends, the cleric lowers his mace and pulls an ankh from beneath his robe. Instead of recoiling, the demon becomes enraged. The elephant-sized spider-demon seems to lose all control of itself and attacks fiercely, without regard for its own safety. It slashes madly at the human with its claws and the talons on four of its jagged legs. One talon tears through the chain mail and leaves a jagged line of blood. A claw tears into the left shoulder of the chain mail, sending the circular links flying into the peach clouds surrounding the battle.

Alynn swings the mace in an attempt to drive the demon back. The weapon passes through the spider-demon's body with no effect. Before he can pull the heavy mace back, the demon's reptilian claws tear jagged lines across the cleric's extended arm.

"Think about the mace hitting the creature." Rhea's voice is calm. "This is a place where the thought is as important as the action."

Alynn does as he is told, and his next blow lands with a satisfying thump on the demon's scaly chest.

SPIDER-DEMON
To Hit Alynn: 9   To Be Hit: 8   Hit Points: 14
Damage per round: 2 D6

The spider-demon has the first attack.

If Alynn survives, turn to section 124.

If Alynn is killed, turn to section 29.

130

The glowing blue globe's appearance is so unexpected that all three humans watch unmoving while the light takes on a vaguely human form. Alynn presses against the wall, further torturing his already battered back and puts up an arm to protect himself from the glowing figure. The blue form reaches down and touches him. For a brief instant he has the impression the figure itself is also in great agony. The form's vague features are contorted and its mouth half open as if screaming silently. Then the pain of Alynn's back diminishes.

New pink flesh appears where moments earlier there were only shreds of charred skin and muscle. The cleric still feels some pain from the burn, but nothing near the mind-numbing torture of crisped muscle and flayed flesh. Looking up, Alynn sees only the black ceiling, the glowing figure has vanished. Glancing around, he can see the shock fade from the face of the man in front of the Gate. Even as he watches, his opponent begins a new conjuration. His expression is no longer one of amused superiority. The cleric pulls himself into a crouch and stumbles toward the gesturing figure.

Turn to section 108.

131

The cleric pulls the scroll from the silver case. Nervously he unrolls the parchment and tries to read it. To his dismay, he sees that the paper is blank. He has already used one spell it would grant. If the solution was here, it is lost.

If Alynn should leave the abbey in pursuit of Lyla, turn to section 122.

If Alynn should use his mace to destroy the runes on the wall, turn to section 117.

Section 132

132

A cry of rage fills the room. The form of the demon is clearer now. The demon is much taller than the human, though more slightly built. Its thin neck seems hardly capable of supporting so massive a head. The head itself is dominated by tiny eyes and a grotesque, tooth-filled beak. The demon's hands end in daggerlike claws. Blood from the wound on its head drips pale green on the glossy black floor, sizzling wherever it falls.

The deadly contest continues for several minutes. Finally, Alynn is able to swing his mace against the creature's spindly neck. With an audible crunch he smashes the heavy weapon into its throat. The demon's war cries are replaced by a whistling gurgle. Backing away, the cleric waits for the demon to fall.

Instead, the enchanted monster rears up to its full height. It charges the cleric, and for a few seconds

Section 133

Alynn can do nothing but dodge a flurry of frantic attacks. Then, just as unexpectedly, the demon topples over. It dissolves moments later into yellow dust, which then vanishes.

For several minutes the battered cleric can only stand and pant. Then the air begins to shimmer. To Alynn's horror the sparks begin to form the outline of a second, identical demon.

If Alynn should continue to try to smash the wall, turn to section 118.

If Alynn should attempt to use a spell off the mummy's scroll, turn to section 133.

If Alynn should leave the abbey in pursuit of Lyla, turn to section 122.

133

The cleric pulls the scroll from its silver case. His eye stops at the incantation to summon an earthquake. If the entire wall is destroyed or if this cavern collapses, the Gate will be inaccessible. The Ankh will no longer be a threat; it won't matter if Lyla has it or not. There is only one disadvantage: Alynn will have to hurry out once the spell is completed or else he will be crushed to death under the ruins. It would be an unfortunate irony to have survived all the perils of the quest only to die as a result of his own actions.

Edging closer to the door, the cleric mouths the first mystic word when he hears the demon's cry. It comes from very nearby. Searching the room anxiously, Alynn notices a sparkling in the air a few steps away. Even as he watches, the sparks form the outline of a vulture-demon. He has only seconds before the creature fully materializes.

If Alynn should put away the scroll and get in the best position to fight the vulture-demon, turn to section 94.

If Alynn should continue to read the chant from the scroll, turn to section 134.

Section 134

134

Trying hard to ignore the materializing form of the demon, Alynn hurries through the unfamiliar spell. He can feel the immense power of the enchantment build as he recites the ancient phrases. His body feels as if suddenly energized, and looking down at his hands, he is almost surprised no sparks dance from his fingertips. Reading the last phrase, the cleric turns his back on the still forming vulture-demon and points at the wall.

"Through the anger of the hunter and the strength of the Protector, let the earth tear itself asunder!"

Cracks appear in the granite blocks. The room shivers, and popping noises announce cracks in the polished floor and ceiling. One of the pillars begins to shift.

The rumble of the quake grows louder. Alynn stands, astonished at the growing power of the enchantment, amazed at what he has done, until a thick block of stone crashes close to him. Looking up, he sees the ceiling split. Tons of earth are about to fall. He dashes for the door, dodging and jumping over opening chasms.

As he hurries from the room, the cleric has the satisfaction of seeing the wall containing the runes crumble. A few feet from it the demon finally completes its materialization only to be caught below an entire section of roof as it caves in. Then a trickle of pebbles warns Alynn that even the cavern is not safe. He remembers the tunnel lined with rotted timbers. It leads up to the abbey. Racing through the tunnel, the cleric hears it collapsing behind him as the earthquake continues to grow in intensity.

Only when Alynn is safely outside the gate of the abbey does he stop running and lean on the wall of the graveyard. From there he observes the temple cave into itself. A section of the wall to the left of the abbey's entrance collapses into a chest-high pile of rubble. He can feel the uneasy earth still shifting beneath his feet, but the worst seems over. Still it is long minutes before the ground is once more peaceful. The cleric watches uneasily, but no demon emerges from the rubble. He hopes it perished in the tunnels below.

Turn to section 116.

135

The sudden return of gravity drags Alynn toward the side of the portal. He tries to twist away but is thrown against the rim behind him. His entire body stiffens as a strip of skin from his back vanishes into the primal ether. His yell of agony echoes through the abbey as the cleric reenters the material plane.

Alynn will receive 1 D6 of damage from contact with the edge of the portal. Subtract this from his total on the record sheet.

If Alynn survives, turn to section 106.

If Alynn is killed, turn to section 29.

136

As he passes beyond the edge of the well, Alynn feels himself snap back into his physical body. Behind him, the well is a diminishing spot, soon lost among the swirling colors.

"Well, you made it." Rhea seems pleased and relieved.

"Didn't you expect me to?"

"It was your only chance," she evades, and then hurries on. "There is something similar ahead, but much less dangerous. You may wish to use it."

"What is that?" Alynn asks. He is less than eager to face another such menace.

"A gap that leads back into your plane." The woman's voice sounds reassuring. "Yours is an established universe, and the danger is minimal. Besides, the gap is much smaller."

"How much smaller?" he asks suspiciously.

"Don't you trust me?"

The cleric floats, supported by nothing, as he looks around at the swirls of color. "I don't have much choice."

Section 136

"You always do," Rhea answers curtly. "It's just that some of the choices aren't very pleasant.... The gap is about the size of the palm of your hand."

Alynn worries he has insulted Rhea. Without her help he has no chance to survive or return to Terverni. Nor has she ever promised, he realizes, that he *can* ever return. Only that he can prevent the Demon Gate from being used.

"You can, if you do what I say," Rhea informs him.

He had forgotten she can read his mind. Their communication seems so natural in this strange environment. With a start, Alynn is reminded how unusual his relationship with Rhea is. How little he knows about the woman—or the entity—behind the voice.

"The portal is just ahead," her voice warns.

A slightly darker spot in the ether is visible ahead. Having learned caution, the cleric slows his progress and approaches carefully. The opening is so small he nearly drifts past it.

On the other side of the fist-sized hole, the man can see sunlight. It looks wonderfully familiar. Willing himself to circle the tiny gap, he is able to see a white stone wall and several square stones set among yellowed grass.

He is looking into a graveyard.

"Yes, now watch the gate," Rhea advises.

A man is entering the graveyard. He is wearing the robe of a priest of Cearn and walks as if exhausted. A mace trails loosely from his right hand. As Alynn watches, the man pauses in the arched entrance and turns to one side. A dark-clad woman joins him.

Lyla! The woman is Lyla.

"And the man?" the voice prompts.

"Me, that's me before we entered the abbey."

"You can try to warn yourself, if you wish."

"You mean I can go back through here?" Alynn inquires hopefully.

"Not really, but you can send a part of yourself. If you can stand the pain."

"Pain?"

"Your ethereal body was never meant to exist on that plane without the protection of a physical shell. That appealing sunlight, those breezes you want to

Section 136

feel, every touch will cause excruciating pain."

The cleric considers the risk. It will be worth a little discomfort if he can warn his earlier self about Lyla's betrayal.

"I'll do it."

"Then concentrate on flowing through that portal. Picture yourself hovering in the air. Remember, I warned you how much it will hurt. Don't let go, whatever you do."

"Let go of what?" he wonders, but Rhea doesn't reply.

At first Alynn cannot break free of his body. Then he is floating over himself, or at least his body, which looks rather battered and abused. The cleric has to resist the automatic impulse to feel pity for the man below him, since that man is himself. His body in turn is floating in the ether over a small sky-colored circle. He looks down to see if this body is floating naked or if there are other two sets of his clothes and armor.

He sees nothing. It seems he has no body.

"No, you have no form here," Rhea agrees. "You have to hurry. In this form you are vulnerable to some very unpleasant creatures that may wander by at any moment. One is very close."

Heeding the warning, the man wills himself through the hole.

Fire! The air feels as if it is flames washing over his body. Looking down, Alynn sees he now has a form of sorts. An ephemeral form that is beginning to shred painfully apart in the slight breeze. The breeze itself feels like knives flaying each part of his roasting skin. With an effort of will, he concentrates on holding himself together.

Only through a haze of pain does he notice the man standing in front of him. He tries to talk, but nothing happens. His form has no vocal cords. Panic rises; he will not be able to warn himself. He is doomed, and so is the world. A second world imposes itself on the first. In it the man conjures and a wave of pain wracks Alynn, then it fades.

He is, the cleric guesses more calmly, half in both planes. Perhaps here, as near the cosmic well, laws from both universes apply. He wills himself to speak

Section 136

and be heard. At first the distraction of the extra task causes his form to be pulled apart by the cutting breeze.

"Pain... This is hard," the words came out as a rustling whisper.

"She will betray you below the abbey," the words came harder, barely distinguishable from the murmur of the breeze.

He finally masters himself just as Lyla reaches his earlier self's side.

"Lyla is much more than she seems," he hurries to add. A small leaf has been lifted on the breeze and drifts through his head. It feels as if hot irons are being jammed into his eyes. He cannot bear to stay any longer. With relief, he flows back through the hole and into his waiting body.

It takes a moment for Alynn to get reoriented. His nerves still tingle from the pain. When he becomes aware of his surroundings again, he sees that the gap to earth is gone. He looks himself over carefully, but there is no new damage.

His first reaction is that he has drifted away from the hole. Painful as it was, the gap was a link to the earth. Frantically he flits about, hoping to catch sight of it.

"It's gone," Rhea says, interrupting his search. "Such gaps rarely last long."

"How could it open to the past, and to that moment in particular?" In retrospect the coincidence seems almost too great to accept. For a panicky moment Alynn worries he is really back at the abbey, delirious. Maybe all this is a terrible nightmare.

"If you don't get going, you will meet a nightmare," Rhea warns. "Something terrible is coming, and I can do nothing to protect you from it."

"What is it?" Alynn asks urgently. In his mind, images of Phameet's ten tongues and eight legs rise unbidden.

"It is one of that Demon Prince's least powerful minions. One of the minor demons that dwell near here. Such creatures are dangerous, but I can suggest one thing you might do immediately."

"Which is?"

Section 136

"Time is different here. You can now renew your devotions to Cearn. You can replenish your store of miracles."

"Can Cearn hear me?" the cleric wonders. "Does he know I am here... wherever *here* is?"

"Cearn hears you as clearly as I do," Rhea reassures and then continues, sounding mildly insulted. "Don't you believe your god knows where his clerics are?"

"He wasn't much help to the other brothers," Alynn snaps back bitterly.

"Some things are beyond even the power of gods," Rhea answers, softly. "Prepare yourself."

At this point you may choose three new spells for Alynn from pages 20–21. See the rules at the front of this book for the procedure. When you have obtained these spells, erase those taken earlier, whether used or not, but not those on the scroll, and list the new ones on the record sheet in their place. If cures are taken, they can be cast now or during any combat.

The cleric is finishing his devotions when he begins to feel he is no longer alone. Willing himself to spin around, Alynn is confronted with a towering figure.

The sight of this lesser demon makes Alynn realize the danger of a Demon Prince loose in the Empire. This lesser demon stands three times the cleric's height and is made of equal parts of spider and lizard. The creature's spider body is a deep blue, broken by bursts of yellow and red. Its eight legs are glossy black, ending in bony points.

It looks like a perverse centaur. Attached to the forward part of the spider body are the chest, arms, and head of a hideously scarred lizardman whose oversized hands are tipped with ivory claws. The spider's legs move as if walking, although the creature seems to float through the almost-clouds.

Neither speaks as man and demon circle each other. An unspoken enmity between the cleric of Cearn and the tool of chaos is sufficient cause for battle. Each knows the other means death. The cleric suddenly wonders if his mace will work on this strange plane. Before he can decide, the demon stops circling and

moves directly toward him. Its lizard face splits in a toothy smile.

If Alynn should cast his Spirit Hammer spell, turn to section 25.

If Alynn should cast a Turn Undead spell, turn to section 129.

If Alynn should cast a Sanctuary spell, turn to section 127.

If Alynn should close in and fight the demon, turn to section 121.

137

Consciousness returns in painful surges. For several minutes Alynn lies there with his eyes closed trying to decide where he was hurt. Finally he decides he hurts everywhere. Whatever had guarded that doorway had affected all of him. It was an effort of will just to open his eyes.

The cleric is rewarded for his effort by the pleased look on Lyla's face. Her expression changes to one of concern as she asks, "Are you okay?"

It takes Alynn several attempts before he can speak clearly. Finally he manages to stammer that he is weak, but expects to live. When he tries to stand, the world spins and Lyla has to support him. Absently, the man tells himself he should appreciate being held so close by such a desirable woman. He wishes he felt strong enough to enjoy the experience. When the cleric's strength returns the sense of urgency returns also. Pulling himself upright, he examines the way ahead.

Turn to section 76

138

The creaking of the hinge wouldn't even have been audible in a crowded room. In the silence of the underground chamber it echoes loudly. Alynn and Lyla tense waiting. Both feel exposed in light pouring through the partially opened door ahead of them.

Section 138

The chanting stops. A threat-filled silence lasts for seconds. Alynn's mind races. He has to enter the room and stop the gate from being opened. Almost before deciding he has no other choice, Alynn dives through the door, smashing it open with his shoulder. It bangs loudly against the wall. The blue-clad man spins and begins gesturing rapidly.

Turn to section 115.

You are the key to the entire story

SWORDQUEST™

Enter the magical realm of SWORDQUEST™—where every hero you've ever wanted to be or know lives at the call of your imagination. Written by Bill Fawcett, a life-long gaming enthusiast, the SWORDQUEST™ novels are also challenging games. Instead of just reading the exciting adventures, you decide when to use your magic, when to fight, when to run, and who should live or die!

__ 0-441-69715-1	Quest for the Unicorn's Horn	$2.95
__ 0-441-69709-7	Quest for the Dragon's Eye	$2.95
__ 0-441-13807-1	Quest for the Demon Gate	$2.95

Prices may be slightly higher in Canada.

Available at your local bookstore or return this form to:

ACE
THE BERKLEY PUBLISHING GROUP, Dept. B
390 Murray Hill Parkway, East Rutherford, NJ 07073

Please send me the titles checked above. I enclose _____. Include $1.00 for postage and handling if one book is ordered; add 25¢ per book for two or more not to exceed $1.75. CA, IL, NJ, NY, PA, and TN residents please add sales tax. Prices subject to change without notice and may be higher in Canada.

NAME _____
ADDRESS _____
CITY _____ STATE/ZIP _____
(Allow six weeks for delivery.)

Stories of Swords and Sorcery

☐ 76600-5	**SILVERGLASS,** J.F. Rivkin	$2.95
☐ 38553-2	**JHEREG,** Steven Brust	$2.95
☐ 11452-0	**CONAN,** Robert E. Howard	$2.95
☐ 81653-3	**TOMOE GOZEN** Jessica Amanda Salmonson	$2.75
☐ 13897-7	**DAUGHTER OF WITCHES** Patricia C. Wrede	$2.95
☐ 10264-6	**CHANGELING,** Roger Zelazny	$2.95
☐ 79197-2	**SWORDS AND DEVILTRY** Fritz Leiber	$2.75
☐ 81466-2	**TO DEMONS BOUND** **(Swords of Raemllyn #1)** Geo. W. Proctor and Robert E. Vardeman	$2.95
☐ 04913-3	**BARD,** Keith Taylor	$2.95
☐ 89644-8	**WITCH BLOOD,** Will Shetterly	$2.95

Prices may be slightly higher in Canada

Available at your local bookstore or return this form to:

ACE
THE BERKLEY PUBLISHING GROUP, Dept. B
390 Murray Hill Parkway, East Rutherford, NJ 07073

Please send me the titles checked above. I enclose _____. Include $1.00 for postage and handling if one book is ordered; add 25¢ per book for two or more not to exceed $1.75. CA, IL, NJ, NY, PA, and TN residents please add sales tax. Prices subject to change without notice and may be higher in Canada.

NAME_____
ADDRESS_____
CITY_____ STATE/ZIP_____
(Allow six weeks for delivery.)